Dark
Secrets 3

ALSO BY
ELIZABETH CHANDLER

Kissed by an Angel

Dark Secrets 1

Dark Secrets 2

Dark Secrets 3

The Back Door of Midnight

ELIZABETH CHANDLER

SIMON AND SCHUSTER

For Brenda and Sharyn

A pulse book

First published in Great Britain in 2011 by
Simon & Schuster UK Ltd,
1st Floor, 222 Gray's Inn Road, London WC1X 8HB
A CBS COMPANY

Published in the USA in 2010 by Simon Pulse,
an imprint of Simon & Schuster Children's Division, New York.

A CIP catalogue record for this book
is available from the British Library

ISBN 978-1-47111-563-9

10 9 8 7 6 5 4 3 2 1

Printed in the UK by CPI Group (UK) Ltd, Croydon, CR0 4YY

One

IT BEGAN AFTER midnight with a low hum, an electric buzz like that of a bass guitar string. The sound grew louder and I tried to cover my head with a pillow, but my arms, heavy with sleep, wouldn't move.

I struggled to sit up; I was paralyzed. Frightened, I tried to call out, but my mouth wouldn't move. An odd sensation began in my feet and traveled up my body, each nerve ending tingling with electric energy. *Stop!* I thought. *Please stop!*

Anna. Let go.

It was a woman's voice that spoke to me, a familiar voice, but I didn't know where or when I had heard it. *Years ago,* I thought. Struggling to recall the person, I momentarily forgot my fear.

The vibrations stopped, and I stood up. I was surrounded by darkness. In the distance an orange light shone. As I moved toward it, I heard a confusion of voices, people talking and laughing. The orange light flickered, and I heard crackling sounds. I could smell now—acrid smoke. I was at a fire.

An object whistled close to my ears and exploded, glass against metal. A siren wailed. I heard feet—heard, rather than saw clearly, people running, panicking. I panicked too. I didn't know who these people were or which way to turn, but instinct told me to get away from there. Then I heard someone else calling my name, a man this time. My uncle was calling to me from the fire.

Anna, be careful.

There were more sirens, the wailing growing closer.

Anna, be careful.

Uncle Will? I answered, moving in the direction of his voice.

The fire surrounded me. I could see the flames like clothing on me, yet I felt no pain, no burning. I reached out my hand, then pulled it back in horror. I had seen through it. I slowly put out my left hand, then my right: They were transparent. Was I dead? Was it possible to die and not know it?

Help! I called out. *Help! Uncle Will! I want to go home.*

I was plucked out of the ghostly fire, reeled in like a fish. Opening my eyes, I found myself in bed at home. The two beds next to mine were empty.

"Grace? Claire?"

Silence.

Then I saw my suitcase and remembered: The twins, Jack, and Mom had left early that morning. I was alone. Next to my suitcase was a plastic bag filled with summer clothes, enough for two months away. I had been dreaming—*obviously*—and yet I would have sworn that I had actually heard Uncle Will's voice. A letter from him lay on top of my suitcase.

I knew the letter by heart, but I climbed out of bed and carried it to the window, pushing back the curtain, unfolding the paper to read by the orange light of a streetlamp.

May 23

Dear Anna,

Would you visit us this summer? The sooner the better. Aunt Iris is doing poorly, and there are things I must tell you about your mother and our family. I want to do so while I am still clear-minded.

Uncle Will

My uncle's invitation had come as a surprise. Eighteen years ago, he and his sister, Iris, both single, had taken in my birth mother, who was pregnant with me. Joanna died in a violent robbery when I was three, and I continued to live with my great-aunt and great-uncle for two more years, before I was adopted by Kathryn, the only person I think of as "Mom."

Since then, Great-Uncle Will had stayed in touch with me by traveling to Baltimore once a year. He didn't like cities, but liked communicating by telephone and computer even less. I loved him and he loved me; still our conversations were awkward.

I never heard from Great-Aunt Iris. When I was older it was explained to me that she was not the most stable person in the world—apparently she heard voices and claimed to be psychic. Until now I had never been asked back to the O'Neill home on Maryland's Eastrn Shore—perhaps to protect me from bad memories of my birth mother's death.

The truth was, I remembered Joanna only through her photos. *My* family was Jack, age seven; Grace and Claire, six; and our dog, Rose—all of us adopted by Mom, living in a skinny brick town house.

There were lots of days I had dreamed of escaping our crowded home; now, having achieved a college scholarship that would allow me to do that, I was getting sentimental over sticky hugs, dog hair, even the sharp little Barbie shoes and Matchbox cars left in my bed. I wanted to spend the summer with my family, but I felt I owed it to Uncle Will, and maybe to Aunt Iris, to visit.

Besides, I was curious. With my brain crammed full of chemistry and calculus, world history and lit, maybe it was time to learn something never asked on the SATs: who I was.

Two

THREE DAYS LATER I drove the highway and then country routes with my windows up, AC blasting, and radio blaring, hoping to drown out the roar of a muffler going bad. In my junior year I had bought what I could afford: a ten-year-old Taurus, an old-man kind of car. Once maroon, now faded grape, it was covered with decals from two previous owners, guys with a taste for hard rock. Since the car couldn't look any worse, I had allowed the twins and Jack to add their own stickers, meaning I traveled with SpongeBob, Batman, Rapunzel Barbie, and Sleeping Beauty. Otherwise, it was a car that any girl would be proud to drive.

Uncle Will had mailed directions to the O'Neill home, which was on the other side of the crek from the town of Wisteria. Missing the driveway on my first pass, I crossed Oyster Creek two more times, then yanked the steering wheel to the right when I saw what looked like "first driveway from the bridge." I was surprised at how nicely Uncle Will kept the entrance, then I came to the cars lining the landscaped driveway and knew I had to be in the wrong place. I cruised up to a manse. Pausing for a moment to gawk at it, I spotted a girl and a guy at the edge of its neat cobblestone circle. They could have been on a poster for a summer blockbuster: hot girl in gorgeous guy's arms, their faces close together and turned toward the camera, her face streaked with tears. Like an actress using glycerin drops, this girl looked amazing in her distress. We stared at one another for what seemed like a full minute.

My passenger-side window didn't work, so I leaned across the seats to push open the door. At the same time the guy circled behind the car, studying the decals and bumper stickers. Having given the kids permission to decorate, I could hardly ban my mother from displaying her political beliefs: OBAMA FOR PRESIDENT, NO TO THE DEATH PENALTY, SAVE THE ORANGUTANS. . . .

The blockbuster girl dried her tears with her long dark hair (a dramatic move, but, unfortunately, he missed it) and joined the guy at my window. I turned off the car so we could hear one another.

"Well," said the girl, "*whose* car did you borrow?"

"It's mine."

The guy smiled a little. "Are you lost?"

"Looks that way."

"Where are you trying to go?"

"The O'Neill house."

The girl's eyes widened, and she exchanged a glance with the guy.

He said, "Of course. I should have guessed. You've got the red hair."

"Chestnut," I replied a little too quickly.

Smiling, he studied it, not arguing, just looking. "And what color do you call your eyes?" His were a stormy blue with dark lashes—incredible eyes, and I figured he knew it. I also figured he knew the attention he was giving me would irk his girlfriend.

"Hazel, obviously."

"Obviously." He laughed.

"Can you give me directions?"

"It's just next door," he said. "At the top of our driveway, go left. The entrance to their property is halfway between here and the bridge, but it's hard to find—overgrown, with no number or mailbox. When you do find it, go real slowly. Their driveway is mostly ruts and shells."

"Yes, be careful," the girl said. "You wouldn't want to damage that car."

"Thanks," I replied, looking at the guy, not her, then starting up the car, its roar ending the possibility of further conversation.

He must have watched my car as I drove the cobblestone circle, for he suddenly ran out in front of me, waving his arms. I wasn't turning off the car again—if he wanted to talk to me, he would have to shout.

"Do you know you're dragging your muffler?"

"Sure sounds like it," I hollered back, and drove on, not that I didn't appreciate his thoughtfulness in telling me, but I saw no point in stopping for a closer look. His clothes were casual chic, laid-back rich-kid clothes, and I was pretty sure he wasn't going to crawl under and take care of it. I could drag it another quarter mile or so.

Back on Scarborough Road, I found what looked like a pull-off rather than a driveway and, after a moment of indecision, left my car there, not wanting to lose a wheel as well as a muffler. The entrance to the rest of the driveway was hidden by a sharp turn and overgrown shrubs. Scrub pine, high grass, and weeds cooked in the late-afternoon heat. About thirty feet beyond was the dense green of trees, and somewhere beyond their leafy darkness lay a house I vaguely remembered. As I walked, the stillness of the Sunday afternoon was eroded by the sound of insects swarming up from the tall grasses. The moment I entered the trees, the air changed, its temperature dropping, its dampness coating my skin.

Patch by patch, the old house began to show through the leaves, pieces of brown shingle roof and weathered gray boards. Its wood had a greenish tinge, like that of the moss-covered trees. I had remembered the house as being unusually long, and when I got close, I saw why. It must have been built as two structures, the left one added on to the right. Both sections of the house had a second floor, but the right portion was taller, boxier. The left portion sat low, with a simple sloping roof and dormer windows for its second floor. A narrow covered porch ran along the front of the low portion.

The house's windows were open, blackened screens in each one, but not a sound came from within. I was relieved to see Uncle Will's pickup parked at the end of the driveway, next to what looked like a horse trailer.

"Hey. . . . Hi. . . . Uncle Will?" I called.

At first I heard only insects, then there were soft, leafy sounds, stirrings in the trees and bushes around me, and cats began to emerge. They strode out in that fluid, stealthy way cats have, their increasing number making them bold. I stopped counting at sixteen.

Several of the cats trotted up the steps to a square porch and sat looking at the entrance to the tall section of the house.

I followed them, opened a warped screen door, then knocked loudly on the main one. There was no answer, and after a moment the cats turned to me expectantly.

"Uncle Will? Aunt Iris?" I knocked again, then turned the handle. The door swung inward, sweeping over a threadbare rug, letting out a breath of musty air. I stepped inside, and so did the cats, padding softly. A center hall ran past the stairs to a door at the back of the house. That door was open, and through it, I could see tall grass, a yard that sloped down to the wide creek.

I called out several times, then noticed the cats scurrying to the front door, which they scratched energetically. After letting them out, I watched the entire herd trot over to Uncle Will's truck. They leaped onto the pickup, some of them choosing to sit on the hood, others making a second leap to the top of the cab. I stepped onto the porch, surveying the trees, wondering what had caused them to act that way.

About a minute later I heard a car engine. An old sedan came barreling through the trees. Branches snapped back and crunched beneath its wheels. When the car stopped next to the pickup, I saw a bouquet of twigs attached to its bumper and another one stuck in its windshield wipers. Perhaps the cats knew from experience to stay clear of this driver.

A tall, broad-boned woman got out of the sedan. Aunt

Iris, I realized. Her hair was dyed a harsh version of its original red, and her skin looked both paler and more freckled than I remembered. In some places it stretched over her large bones; in others, like the backs of her arms, it hung loose.

"Oh, stop it!" she snapped, before I could speak a word. "I've heard enough already."

She stalked toward the porch where I stood, but never looked at me. I assumed she was talking to the cats, since they had jumped down from the truck and were mewing. Then her gaze became fixed on the right porch post.

"Hello, Aunt Iris."

She turned her head sharply. For a moment she looked surprised to see me, then she made a face. "It's about time!"

I glanced at my watch. "I told Uncle Will three o'clock."

"Well, he didn't tell me. He didn't even mention you were coming back."

"He didn't?" *Uh-oh.* "Where is Uncle Will?"

"At the coroner's—most of him, that is."

"Excuse me?"

"They won't return him. They said they have more tests to do. It's not right, a man to be half ashes, half skin. He should be one or the other."

I stared at her, a grisly image materializing in my head. "Half ashes . . . you mean he's dead?"

She nodded and looked somewhat smug. "I see you didn't know. That's William for you—always forgetting to mention the important things."

"When did he die?" I cried. "How did he die?"

She shot a look at the right porch post. "You'll have to ask him yourself. He's not speaking to *me*."

I glanced at the post as if I might see him there, then back at her. She wasn't making sense—not that anyone claiming that my uncle was dead would have made sense to me. Had he been seriously ill and waiting till I got here to tell me?

Then I got a creepy feeling. *Half ashes.* "Was there a fire?"

"Of course there was a fire," she replied, stomping up the steps and into the house.

I followed her, images from my dream flickering through my mind. "Were other people there? Were there kids my age? Did someone deliberately set the fire?"

"You ask too many questions, Joanna."

"Anna," I corrected quietly.

"What?" She spun around, and I stepped back.

She was a head taller than I, and her hands, though worn, were still powerful, like those of a woman who had spent her life working a farm. I had no problem imagining her snapping the necks of chickens before throwing them in a boiling pot.

"I'm Anna, Anna O'Neill Kirkpatrick. Joanna was my mother," I said. "She's dead, remember?"

"Despite what William says, I remember everything that I want to."

She strode through the dining room. I trailed her, and two kitties trailed me.

"Why aren't you in Baltimore?" Aunt Iris asked, making it clear she now knew who I was.

"Uncle Will invited me. He said there were some family things he wanted to talk about."

I saw the color wash up the back of her neck. She shoved the swinging door between the dining room and kitchen so hard, it slammed against the kitchen wall. "He wanted to talk about *me*. He thinks I'm out of my mind. He thinks I should be committed to the crazy-people place."

I caught the door as it bounced back at me. The two cats slinked away.

"I've been there," Iris went on, "and I just can't get along with those people. They're strange."

"I guess so." I glanced around the room, which had appliances even older and stickier-looking than ours and a faded tile floor. Perhaps when you are less than three feet tall, you stare at the floor a lot: The checkerboard pattern was familiar to me.

"What do you see?" Aunt Iris asked.

"Excuse me?"

"What do you see?" she demanded, sounding almost fearful.

It took me a moment to catch on. If a porch post looked like Uncle Will's ghost to her . . . "Nothing but a kitchen," I replied. "A stove, sink, cupboards. Aunt Iris, what day did Uncle Will die?"

She looked at me out of the corner of her eye. "I don't know."

Apparently, it was one of those things she chose not to remember.

She dropped down in a chair, her sandaled feet spread wide apart and loose dress gaping between her knees. "I'm exhausted. Stupid deputy. It's indecent to keep a man half skin and half ashes."

I sat down with her at the kitchen table.

"Fix yourself something to drink," she said. "I don't have Mr. Pepper."

"You mean Dr Pepper?"

"For the love of God!" she exploded. "People expect everything from a psychic! 'Doctor,' 'mister,' I was close enough. I didn't call it 'Mrs. Salt,' did I?"

"No. No, you didn't. Water is perfect," I said, though in fact I had been longing for a Dr Pepper and found it creepy that she knew.

I rose and filled a glass from the tap, then walked over to the freezer for ice cubes. Opening the door, I jumped back. A large, speckled fish—scales, fins, head, and tail—tumbled out, landing at my feet. I stared down at it, then up at the compartment, which was filled with fish.

"Put it back, put it back!" Aunt Iris cried.

I quickly stuffed the fish in with the others and decided I could do without the ice cubes.

"So Uncle Will is—was—still fishing a lot," I observed.

"I can't stand the way they look at you. So accusingly!"

"The fish, you mean, their glassy eyes?"

"The fire was Wednesday night."

The sudden disclosure caught me by surprise. *The same night as my dream*, I thought, my sweaty skin feeling cold. I sat down at the table again.

"Where did it happen?"

"Near Tilby's Dream—the old farm. The car's been rusting there for years," she added. "Sheriff said it took some work to pry open the trunk."

"Uncle Will was inside the trunk?"

She nodded. "Poor William, he hated Buicks. He always insisted on Chevrolets."

"Did someone . . . put him there—did someone kill Uncle Will?" I asked.

"I *said* he hated Buicks. You don't think he climbed in willingly, do you?"

"No," I said slowly, "not even if he liked the car."

Obviously, Aunt Iris was not the most reliable source of information. I had to talk to the police—the sheriff, she had said. Then what? If my great-aunt was losing it mentally, what was I supposed to do? Mom would know; but she would come rushing home from a vacation she needed badly. I could handle this—at least for a little while, I could.

"How long are you going to stay?" Aunt Iris asked.

"I'm not sure. I have college orientation—"

"Your clothes are in Papa's room, in the mahogany bureau."

"Oh!" I visualized myself in a kindergartner's clothes. "I don't think I'll fit them anymore."

"Well, don't expect me to buy you any. We're going to need every penny for the child."

"What child?"

"She'll be here soon enough."

I gazed at my great-aunt, mystified. Then I realized I must have slipped back into being Joanna. My mother was attending college when I was born. The child who was coming was probably myself, and she had been speaking of my mother's clothes in the mahogany bureau.

When Uncle Will had written that Aunt Iris was doing poorly, he wasn't kidding. Was she senile or just plain crazy?

Her eyes met mine. "You would be crazy too, if you saw and heard the things I do."

I took a long sip of water. Had she just read my thoughts? No. She had heard herself talking and, knowing that she didn't make sense, had offered an explanation.

When I glanced up, her eyes were darting around the room, as if insects were popping out of the kitchen walls and she was trying to count them. Her eyes finally lit on me.

"I'm Anna," I said, just in case.

"Then I suppose you've brought luggage."

"It's in my car at the top of the driveway," I replied, although, at the moment, I was thinking about finding a motel.

She stood up. "You may as well fetch it and start unpacking. William knows you're here."

Perhaps he can knock twice to say hello, I thought. Aunt Iris was one person I wouldn't want to join in a séance.

She gave me a sideways look. "Unless you're afraid of me. You were as a child."

"I'm not now. I'll get my things."

After placing my glass in the sink, I retraced my steps through the dining room to the center hall and front door. When I had exited and looked back at the house, I realized I could have left directly from the kitchen. It was the first room in the long, low section of the house, and Aunt Iris was watching me from behind its screen door.

I trudged up the gradual incline to my car, feeling her eyes in my back even when the curtain of trees was between us. I drove slowly toward the house, trying to avoid ruts and cats. Easing past Aunt Iris's car, Uncle Will's truck, and the horse trailer, I parked at the far edge of the driveway, snug against some shrubs so I wouldn't be in my aunt's way. I pulled out my suitcase and started toward the house.

There was a sudden roar of an engine, and I leaped back, flattening myself against the pickup truck. Aunt Iris's gold Chevrolet lurched backward, then stopped. I stood on my toes, sandwiched between the sedan and the truck. If I leaned half an inch forward, I'd touch her car. I heard the front wheels wrench around on the shells and dirt, watched its big metal nose turn, and stared after the car as it sped off through the trees. She was a maniac.

I wondered if there was someone besides my uncle looking out for Aunt Iris. I had a bad feeling there wasn't and that she didn't want there to be. The first thing I'd do was charge up my cell phone. I dropped my bag at the bottom of the stairway, then headed into the kitchen, figuring it would have the best outlet. When I saw the stove, I gasped. A burner was on, the gas turned up all the way, with blue flames shooting into the air, looking hungry for something to burn. I ran to the stove and twisted one of its knobs. A window curtain hung just inches from the flames—if a breeze had stirred, it would have caught fire immediately.

Why did she do this? I thought angrily. *Stay cool,* I told myself. There was a teapot on the burner behind the one that had been lit. It was possible that Iris thought she had lit that burner, then decided to leave suddenly and forgot about it—just like it was possible that she never saw me when she backed up the car. Of course, it didn't much matter: Whether by neglect or plan, she was dangerous. I had a credit card and could stay at a cheap highway motel. Still, I hated being cowed by an old lady, my own great-aunt, especially after the challenge she had issued. I'd stay tonight; whether or not I'd sleep was another question.

Three

WITH THAT DECIDED, I opened the refrigerator to see if there was something more than glassy-eyed fish to eat. One look told me that food shopping was a priority. The date on the egg carton indicated that they were laid in March. The lids on the mayo and mustard were off, the mustard's yellow separating from the vinegary part. There was a flounder lying on top of an open butter dish and the tail of another sticking out of the meat drawer. I peeked in the crisper. A package of slimy deli meat sat on a pile of mail. After a moment of debate, I removed the mail.

All of it was addressed to Uncle Will's post office box. Some of it looked like bills—electric, telephone, Visa; the postmarks were from the previous week. I realized that if Aunt Iris kept mail in the fridge as long as she kept other things, she'd need someone to help her with her bills. Did she and Uncle Will have a lawyer or someone else who could do this?

Flipping through the envelopes, I came upon one that was missing a postage stamp and marked RETURN TO SENDER. It was addressed in my uncle's bold handwriting to the Maryland State Police. Adding postage and sending it on would have been the right thing to do, but curiosity got the better of me. I opened it.

Uncle Will was requesting a transcript of all the information the police had collected on the unsolved murder of Joanna O'Neill. He had attached to his letter a copy of a newspaper article, with the date circled.

YOUNG MOTHER KILLED IN ROBBERY, the headline blared. I took a deep breath and read.

> Last Monday evening, twenty-two-year-old
> Joanna O'Neill, niece of William and Iris,
> was found murdered in their home. The
> crime occurred in the living room of the
> O'Neill homestead, "old Doc O's house,"
> as it is commonly called, next to the bridge
> over Oyster Creek. When William O'Neill
> and young Anna, Joanna's three-year-old
> daughter, returned from shopping, William
> noticed that the entrance hall of the home
> was in disarray. After putting the toddler
> back in his truck, he found the bloody body

of Joanna. Rooms on both floors had been ransacked.

According to the coroner, the victim died from blunt force trauma to the head. A pair of silver candleholders and a large amount of cash were taken from the house. No weapon for the murder was found. There was no evidence of forced entry.

Iris O'Neill, William's sister, was visiting a sick friend at the time.

According to Sheriff McManus, Shore residents "aren't in the habit of locking doors, and someone thought he could just walk in and help himself to whatever he wanted."

Joanna O'Neill, who was attending Chase College, hoped to embark on a career in health care. She was known in Wisteria as a psychic and had a loyal clientele for whom she read cards. A Mass of Christian Burial was offered for her last Thursday at St. Mary's Church on Scarborough Road.

My mother read cards? She was psychic like Aunt Iris? Why hadn't Uncle Will told me? Maybe he didn't like the idea.

I slipped the letter and article back in the envelope, feeling strange. I knew I had loved my birth mother—I had seen pictures of us together. But the face I thought of with sadness was Uncle Will's, when he saw the ransacked house, when he put me back in his truck, when he searched and found Joanna dead. The loss I felt from his death was beginning to seep through my initial state of shock, tightening my throat, making me blink back tears.

A loud knock at the front door jolted me out of these thoughts.

"Hello? Anyone home? Hello!"

I wiped my cheeks and blew my nose. Leaving bills and ads on the kitchen table, I carried Uncle Will's letter into the hall, stuffed it in my suitcase, then opened the front door.

"So you found your way." It was the guy from next door, without his hot costar. He held out his hand, a large hand with a silver wristband to show off the tan. "I'm Zack."

"I'm Anna."

Standing face-to-face with him—or rather, face-to-chest; he was about a foot taller than me—I found myself wanting to back up. His eyes were intense and didn't miss a freckle.

After a moment he said, "I see Iris isn't home. Do you know when she'll be back?"

"No, I haven't a clue. She rushed out of here."

He nodded, then glanced toward the vehicles parked at one end of the house. "My stepmother sent me over. She would like something done about the goats on the back lawn."

"The goats?"

"You didn't notice them," he said. "Unfortunately, Marcy did, and she went ballistic. They don't go well with her . . . garden soiree."

"Aunt Iris raises goats?"

"No. They're clients."

For a moment I was puzzled. "Oh, I see. She grooms goats."

"No, she's their therapist, their psychologist."

"You're kidding me!"

"I think the goats take it seriously," he replied, then smiled. "Here's the problem: Marcy wants the goats gone, like, immediately. Perhaps you could talk to their owner—"

I began to shake my head.

"Or the goats, whichever works best," he said, his eyes bright, as if laughing. "Iris usually goes along with what Marcy wants, and while I don't care and Dad doesn't care, Marcy's throwing a major fit."

"Well, if she doesn't want goats ruining her view, maybe she should get a house in town."

"I'm not arguing *that* point. In the meantime, the party's

about to start, and the goats are out back, and my stepmother is about to lose it." He smiled at me, a flirty smile. "Tell you what: If you get rid of them, I'll fix your car."

"You know how to replace mufflers?" I asked, surprised.

"I know how to drive to Midas."

"I thought so. Tell your stepmother I'll ask the owner to take his goats and come back later. But I can't promise he'll listen to me," I added, then closed the front door and headed down the hall to the back entrance. I couldn't believe I was playing receptionist to a pet shrink.

The creek side of the house was just as I remembered it, sunny, with two big trees and a stretch of tall grass between the house and the water. A swath about ten feet wide was mowed around the house and ran in a path down to the dock. Two goats were grazing, watched over by a man who sat with his back against a willow.

As I approached the man, one of the goats raised its head and gazed at me with interest. The other kept its head down but didn't eat. The owner, whose round, pleasant face made me think of a worn catcher's mitt, nodded at me, then, realizing I wanted to speak to him, rose quickly to his feet.

"Afternoon, miss," he said with a soft drawl, a Shore accent like my uncle's.

"Hi. Listen. I'm sorry, but I need to ask you to take your goats somewhere else. My aunt Iris isn't home and—"

"She'll be back," he said with certainty. "We had an appointment."

"Yes. Yes, I'm sure you did, but, you know, she doesn't remember things as well as she used to."

"Happens to all of us," he said, smiling in that tolerant way an adult smiles at a child who doesn't understand. "But kind of you to let me know," he added, tapping the top of his head as if there were a hat he might tip to me. He sat down again, ready to wait.

"What I'm saying is that I have no idea when she'll be home."

"It's Sunday," he replied. "I'm not much in a hurry."

I doubted he was ever in a hurry. "Unfortunately, the lady next door is having a party, and she doesn't like goats."

"Oh, they'll stay on this side of the hedge."

"I wonder if you could make another appointment?"

He considered the suggestion, then considered me. "You're an O'Neill. You got the red hair."

I bit back the word "chestnut." "Yes, I'm Iris's great-niece."

"They say all the O'Neill women are either psychic or crazy. You don't look crazy." Before I could thank him for that acute observation, he went on. "Maybe you can help me out—do a reading."

He saw the disbelief on my face and added quickly, "Oh, not for me! For Maria. *Maria.* She's having a bad time."

I followed his eyes to a black-and-white goat, the one that was gazing forlornly at the ground but not eating.

"She's not looking good," I admitted.

"You could ask her the problem," he said hopefully. "You could ask her what she would like me to do. I just can't figure out what's botherin' her. Her appetite's off. She's getting nasty with the other goats, even her sister, Daisy, here."

"Did you take her to a vet?"

He nodded. "Can't find anything wrong with her, just her usual dental problems—always had them. I give her special food."

"Well, I'm sorry she's unhappy, but—"

"Maybe you could just get down with her for a minute," he said.

"Get down?"

"Like Iris does. Get down on her level, close your eyes, and listen to her mind."

"But I know nothing about goats. Until now I've only seen them at petting zoos."

"They're not much different than us," he replied. "They just can't speak English. But I understand. I'll wait. Sooner or later, Iris will remember."

I glanced toward the property next door.

A stocky, white-haired woman stood at a tall gate in the

hedge, watching us. She was dressed in black and white, the outfit of a household employee. I wondered if Zack's step-mother had sent her out to see what progress was being made. Well, it wasn't my problem.

But I did feel sorry for Maria and walked over to see if she would let me pet her. When I leaned down to her, she lifted her head slightly. Whew! Talk about bad breath!

"I think you should brush after meals," I said, and moved around to the side of her, where the smell wasn't as strong.

She rolled an eye toward me.

"Not feeling so good, huh?"

She made a soft bleating sound.

"Feeling kind of cranky? And everybody else, instead of being nice to you, gets mad at you because they expect you to be your happy self all the time, like you're just there for them and haven't got any problems of your own?"

Another bleat.

"Iris usually kneels and lays her head against Maria's," the man called to me.

Grateful that my friends in Baltimore couldn't see me, I knelt, but I was not going to put my head against a goat's. *So what is it?* I asked, silently, of course—I'm not crazy.

If I were a goat, why would I be making myself miserable, staying apart from the others? Maybe they were dissing her.

Dental problems gave you bad breath, breath that might be foul even to a sister goat. I studied her skinny little chin.

Are they giving you a hard time about the way you smell? Those mean old goats! And I bet some people haven't been so nice either.

She blinked, and had I believed in psychic connections, I would have thought she had just said *yes*.

Do you like to be petted? I'm not going to hurt you. I reached up, lightly touched her back, then stroked her. She turned to look at me full in the face, and I stopped breathing. Whew!

Guess it has been a while since anyone has wanted to pet you face-to-face. Maybe that's part of the problem—you're feeling unloved, taken for granted. How about if I tell your owner that?

I stood up, opened my mouth to suck in a big gulp of air and snort the smell out of my nose, then walked over to the man beneath the tree.

As I delivered my report, he squinted at the goat and nodded in agreement. "You know, the grandkids have been around a lot since school let out, and they like the goats—the others, not her. Never thought about it till now. She's hurtin' for attention, with that bad breath and all."

From his pocket, he pulled out a cracked leather wallet, and I realized that he was going to pay me. I waved my hand. "No money."

"But I pay Iris," he insisted.

I couldn't take money for making up stuff. "I'm just learning," I said. "I can't take money while I'm learning."

"Well . . . well, I thank you. And Maria thanks you. Come on, you silly girl. I'll give you a nice grooming when we get home."

He herded his goats toward the long end of the house, and I figured the horse trailer parked out front was his. I also figured that Maria's problems would prove easier to solve than Aunt Iris's.

"Nicely done."

I turned quickly and saw Zack sitting on the back step leading to the hall door. As I walked toward him, I could feel my cheeks getting warm, and I willed them not to. "I thought you went home."

He smiled. "No, I walked around the side of the house. I was curious." He jumped up and held open the screen door to the hall. "May I?"

What PBS miniseries had he hatched from? I didn't know a single guy under thirty-five who would hold a door and ask to come in by saying, *May I?*

He followed me into the house. "Are you psychic?" he asked.

"No."

He tilted his head slightly, studying me again, considering my response. His eyes were the same kind of changeable blue as the creek. They were dangerous eyes.

"You're sure?"

"Very. I arrived today expecting my uncle to be alive, hoping to spend a summer with him. That's how psychic I am."

Now his face grew serious. "Oh, God. I'm sorry. I'm really sorry. . . . No one told you?"

"According to Aunt Iris, Uncle Will always forgets to mention the important things." I laughed, but Zack gazed at me, brow furrowed. "That was a joke," I said, "although she really seems to have expected him to inform me of his death."

"No one told your parents?"

I didn't feel like explaining my family. "No."

"Do you want to borrow my cell phone and call someone?" For the first time he was less than smooth. He reached in one pocket then another, fumbling for his phone. "I've got a zillion minutes—"

"No thanks. Mine's charging."

He nodded and put the iPhone back in his pocket. "Will you be staying the summer? Will somebody else be coming to help you?"

"I don't know. My family's on vacation, and I have a lot of things to figure out." I looked up at him, meeting his eyes squarely. "What do you know about my uncle's death?"

Zack didn't move, but I saw him pull back from the question. "What do I know?"

"Aunt Iris says he was burned in the trunk of a car."

"That's what I heard."

"And that it happened Wednesday night."

"It did." He sounded cautious, like a lawyer being interviewed by a TV reporter.

"If you're worried about telling me something gory or morbid, just spill it. I'm going to learn what happened one way or another, the sooner the better."

"I don't know much," he said.

I took a gamble, remembering my dream. "Were some kids there? Was it a party thing?"

"That's what they're investigating. There have been three other fires—arsons—which the police think were set by a group of kids just fooling around."

"Murder's not just fooling around!" The anger in my voice surprised me.

Even with his tan, I saw the red creep into Zack's face. "I didn't mean to imply that."

He was holding back something, I could sense it. He shoved his hands in his pockets. "You should talk with Sheriff McManus. His office is on the corner of Jib and Water Streets. I've got to go now."

"I will talk to him," I said as Zack headed for the door, "but I get the feeling you know something he doesn't."

Turning back for a moment, Zack gave me a half smile. "And you said you weren't psychic."

Four

WHILE AUNT IRIS was out, I checked out the rest of the house, searching for anything that might indicate what had happened to Uncle Will and what he had wanted to tell me.

The living room, full of lumpy chairs with worn fabric, lay to the right of the stairs and center hall. The only thing I remembered in it was the tall grandfather clock. The dining room, to the left of the stairs, was smaller than I recalled. In the center hall, a table hugged the wall beneath a long and tarnished mirror. The phone on the table was old. Lifting the clunky receiver, I heard a reassuring dial tone.

I picked up my suitcase and climbed the steps to the second floor. At the top of the stairway a window overlooked the backyard of the house. To the right was a large bedroom. I remembered its wallpaper, the big, blue mop-headed flowers, but despite the twin beds and crib, I didn't recall sleeping there. My eyes slid over to the mahogany bureau. I told myself I needed to keep checking the house while Aunt Iris was gone, but that was just an excuse for not opening the drawers to see if they contained clothes worn by my birth mother.

On the other side of the stairs and hall were a bath and two bedrooms. The front room, its walls green and shadowy from the press of trees, must have been Aunt Iris's. I remembered its herbal smell, a good smell, but it brought back a feeling of fear. The back room, facing the water, was Uncle Will's. Surveying the simple furniture of his room, my eyes stopped at a door opposite from where I was standing. I knew the moment I saw the door that I used to go through it.

Opening it, I found the entrance to the left side of the house, the portion that lay beneath the sloping roof. A long, low-ceilinged room with bare planking and dormer windows—three facing the water, three facing the trees—it looked like an orphan's dormitory in an old storybook. In the corner closest to Uncle's Will's room, snug against the sloping roof, was the bed where I had slept. I knew it the moment I saw it. Two painted bureaus, a rocking chair, and a child's chair made a cozy little square. It was creepy, everything still in place as if the kindergartner who had slept there would be returning. Of course, I could imagine how it must have looked to the people from Social Services—kid kept in the attic—but I remembered the feeling of warmth and safety I'd had here. I set down my suitcase. This was where I would sleep tonight.

Beyond my little corner were boxes, trunks, miscellaneous pieces of furniture, and a cemetery of television sets. There were ten TVs, most of them the same size, all of them having one obvious feature: a smashed screen. Ten times was nine times too many for an accident, and I doubted it was Uncle Will who had gotten mad.

At the end of the long room was a massive chimney with steps next to it. I crossed the floor quickly and descended a turning staircase to a room full of books. Uncle Will's den—I remembered playing dolls here. The huge fireplace and the brick floor indicated that it was the original kitchen of the homestead. I assumed the police had searched it for clues about Uncle Will's death, but there were so many books and papers that if anything was hidden, it could have easily been missed. I planned to search it too.

At that moment a cat that must have been following me came flying down the corner stairs and clawed at the door to the outside. I glanced at the clock on Uncle Will's desk, then opened the door and listened for a moment. I could hear nothing, but I let the cat out so it could join the other cats, which were leaping onto the hood of Uncle Will's pickup. A minute and a half later the gold car came roaring down the driveway.

I had expected my aunt; still, the skin at the back of my neck prickled at the sight of her. Was the cats' hearing that good, or did she communicate with them in some way?

She climbed out of her Chevrolet and stood with her head cocked, as if she, herself, were listening to something.

"Hello, Aunt Iris," I called before emerging from the house, hoping I wouldn't startle her.

She whipped around.

"It's me, Anna," I said.

She looked hard at me. "I remember. I remember everything that I want to."

The problem was, I had no way of knowing what she did *not* want to.

"A man was here with his goats," I went on. "He said he had an appointment."

"I knew he was here. I had to leave. The voices wouldn't stop."

"The man asked for—for my advice about one of his goats, so I gave it to him."

She nodded, as if it were perfectly normal for me to be making suggestions about farm animals. "Maria gets her feelings hurt easily," she said. Then she blinked and turned her head slowly. I looked where she looked but saw nothing, not even a porch post resembling Uncle Will.

"Stop it!" she said angrily. "I won't listen to you anymore!"

I moved out of the shadow of the house and heard bits of jazzy music mixed with the rise and fall of voices. "The people next door are having a party," I told her.

"Even when they whisper, I can hear them telling me what to do." Her voice quavered with emotion.

"What to do about what?"

"William. You."

"Oh." In Baltimore I might have found this conversation humorous, but here in the gloom of the old house and encroaching trees, it made me uneasy.

"You've been talking to William, haven't you?" she said accusingly. "You were in his den."

I glanced over my shoulder. "I was there, but he wasn't. He's at the coroner's, remember?"

"He never hears the voices."

"I don't hear them either," I told her. "But maybe, if you tell me what they are saying, I can help you figure out where they are coming from and what to do about them."

Her eyes flew wide. "I can't! I can't say a word! There are secrets I can tell no one."

"Secrets about what?"

"I can't tell you!" She sounded panicky and took a step back from me. "Don't ask me, the voices will be angry." She held her ears with her hands. "How they taunt me!" she moaned.

She shook her head from side to side, then dug her index fingers into her ears. "Stop it! Stop it!"

"Aunt Iris—"

She backed against her car. When she started to fall, I rushed forward to catch her. She slid down the side of the car. I struggled to pull her up, but she was dead weight. She sank to the ground, sitting with her knees pulled up to her chest.

"Aunt Iris, everything's okay. Everything's okay."

She bent forward, her head and hands between her knees, as if they could help keep out the maddening voices. I knelt in front of her, my hands clenched, feeling useless.

I wanted to run back to Baltimore—she scared me. But I owed it to Uncle Will to stay. When my mother died, he had taken care of me, giving all he could. Now he had died, leaving someone behind, and it was my turn.

It would take weeks to figure out what Iris needed and how to get it for her. Maybe I could find the medicine she was supposed to take, a bottle with a doctor's name on the label. I had to figure out if she was safe alone—and if others were safe from her when she was left alone.

"Aunt Iris. Aunt Iris, listen to me!" I increased the volume of my voice until I was shouting at her. "There's no one here but me. It's just me."

Finally, she removed her hands from her ears.

"We need to go inside now. I'll fix us something to eat. You'll feel better if you have some dinner."

She looked about, then reached for the car's outside mirror and pulled herself to her feet. "How long will you be staying?" she asked.

"For a while."

"What kind of job will you get? I hope you don't read cards."

"Read cards?" I repeated, surprised. "You mean tell people's fortunes? No way!"

She nodded, brushed something aside with her hand— maybe a cobweb I couldn't see—and headed toward the kitchen door. "Good. Stick to animals, Joanna. People are vicious. They will turn on you."

Five

A SEARCH OF the kitchen cupboards produced a box of macaroni with cheese flakes that could be mixed and cooked, which was filling and safer than the food in the fridge. Aunt Iris ate two mouthfuls, said she wasn't hungry, and retreated to her bedroom. I waited five minutes, then carried her plate upstairs. Her door was closed. I knocked and asked her if she was feeling all right—she was. I asked if she would mind me opening the door—she would. I told her I had brought up her dinner in case she wanted a little more—she didn't.

Returning to the kitchen, I finished mine, then sat on the back stoop, watching the first shy stars appear. I wondered if Zack and his girlfriend had hung around for the party. A hedge about four feet high separated his yard from Aunt Iris's. With no lights burning on the O'Neill property other than the beacon at the end of Uncle Will's dock, I figured no one from the party could see me. I walked halfway down the slope to the water and looked back at the two houses. Aunt Iris's was dark, huddled against the trees. Zack's home was lit like a manse in a movie: lamps shining softly inside the long windows, candles flickering on the patio, torches winding a path down the black velvet lawn, red and gold lanterns on the dock.

I walked down the mowed path to Uncle Will's dock. His boat was missing. A new ladder had been installed on the side of the dock where he used to tie up. I guessed he wasn't as agile as he'd once been.

For some reason, I have always found black water scary. So I sat on the dock with my back to the dark creek and the party, facing the bridge with its old-fashioned lamps and the town twinkling beyond it. Wisteria was surrounded by water on three sides, the Sycamore River and the creeks of Oyster and Wist, creeks that were as wide as the river itself. It was Aunt Iris's and Uncle Will's father who had purchased this old house and property outside of town, next to the bridge over Oyster Creek, a perfect place for him to set up as a large-animal vet who called on farms.

I wondered what it was like to be as old as Aunt Iris, living your whole life in this one house—except for the hospital stays, of course. Had Uncle Will joined the army to get away from the small town, to see the world? Too late now to ask him that. I wondered, if I had come a week earlier, whether I could have kept his death from happening.

The Back Door of Midnight

I sat swinging my legs above the water. The smell of the creek made me think of the summer days I had sat on the dock with him, wearing one of his fishing hats—they must have been his, they always fell over my eyes—each of us holding a rod. I fought back tears. For a moment I thought he was there—actually there—resting a hand on my shoulder. I turned quickly.

At the same time, standing on a dock a hundred feet across the water, Zack turned toward me. The dark-haired girl I had seen earlier leaned against him casually, her head turned away from me. Zack gazed at me, his face thoughtful in the gold light of the lanterns. He looked . . . and looked. I finally glanced down. The dark stretch of creek between us reminded me of just how far apart our worlds were. I rose to my feet and headed back to the house.

After entering the kitchen, it took me a few minutes to find the light switch. A bright kitchen is usually cozy, but with no streetlights around, I found the sudden blaze of light unnerving. I felt like a lit-up window display, unable to see what was outside in the trees. I turned off the light and let my eyes adjust to the darkness. Then I stepped out the front door of the kitchen onto the narrow porch that ran the length of the lower part of the house. I followed it to the end, past Aunt Iris's Chevy, and retrieved a flashlight from my car's emergency kit.

Turning back to the long house, surveying it from end to

end, I saw that the old kitchen, now Uncle Will's den, was connected to the main house by the new kitchen and another room. All the rooms on the left side of the house had a door to the front, facing the trees, and a door to the back, facing the creek. There was one room I hadn't looked in, the one between the old and new kitchens. I walked toward it, shining my light on its entrance.

I found the door locked, and not just the door, but the window, too. I shone my light through it, but I could see only a table and bookshelves. At home, when going to bed, we closed up and locked the windows on the first floor, but it appeared that, with the exception of this one room, Aunt Iris's house was always open. *Oh, well.*

Upstairs, I found the door to Aunt Iris's room still shut. I pressed my ear against it and, hearing nothing, called her name softly.

"William?" she replied, sounding as if she were half asleep.

"No. It's Anna. I'm going to bed now. I'll be in the room next to Uncle Will's, in the bed where I used to sleep, okay?"

She didn't answer, and I wondered if she had fallen back asleep. "Good night," I said quietly.

"Good night."

I changed into my nightshirt, put on clean athletic shorts, and laid a pair of slip-on shoes next to my bed, just in case.

Exhausted by all the emotions of the day, I stretched out on the little bed and stared up at the sloping ceiling. The soft lamp next to my bed cast an arc of light against the low ceiling. I remembered as a child gazing at that particular pattern of light and shadow, staring at it until my eyes were too heavy to stay open.

I awoke to a low throbbing sound. I lay there, eyes closed and listening. I felt anxious, as if some part of me knew what the sound was, knew what would happen next, and didn't want it to. I couldn't move my arms, couldn't roll over to cover my face, couldn't even turn my head to see what or who was next to me. My bed began to shake. A strange, electric energy traveled up my body, taking over me, leaving every muscle, tendon, and nerve tingling.

Stop! Please stop!

And then I remembered the last time, the familiar voice, the calming words: *Anna, let go.*

Let go, let go, I repeated to myself.

The sound and shaking stopped. Able to move, I stood up. I was surrounded by darkness. I looked for the flickering orange light, but it wasn't there, and I began to panic again. "Help me!"

I could speak. I could hear my own voice.

The opaque blackness slowly lightened, as if the moon was

emerging from behind a cloud. I gazed upward and saw an edge to the darkness, like the rim of a high wall. It was traced in silvery light and notched like the battlements of a castle. I lowered my eyes, trying to find the bottom of the blackness, and saw an opening in the wall. If there was a choice, it didn't feel like it to me; I had to go through, and I did.

On the other side of the wall were paths, many of them, but they all went to one place. Two tall figures stood close to me, still as statues. I moved past them, uneasy with the way they seemed to watch me.

Suddenly, the ground gave way. I was falling down a hole. A small light appeared in the distance, and I moved toward it. From my previous dream, I thought I knew where I was headed. I expected to smell fire and hear laughter and talking, but the night was silent. All I could smell was a pinelike sweetness and the sour odor of wet ashes. There was no flickering brightness tonight, just one small bobbing light and a single voice—Aunt Iris talking to herself.

I could see the shape of her, her loose dress and wild hair, but everything was blurry, one form melting into the next. "Aunt Iris, what is going on?"

She tilted her head as if she heard my voice.

"Please," I begged. "I don't know what's happening to me. I can't see very well. Aunt Iris, I need to see."

As soon as I spoke, I saw that the bobbing light was a flashlight. My vision had become clearer, although things still looked strange. I could see police tape in all four directions, as if I were standing in the center of a crime site and had eyes in the sides and back of my head.

The ground beneath me was dark and crusty—scorched, I realized; the car was gone, but this was where it had burned. Aunt Iris sat down, dug her fingers into the ground, and raised her palms, letting the ashy earth sift through her fingers. She looked bizarre, her legs spread out like a little girl's, her hands scooping the soft surface like a child playing in a sandbox. She took a jar from her pocket and unscrewed the lid. After setting it next to her, she continued to sift through the ashy earth. When she found a handful she liked, she put it in the jar.

I watched for several minutes. "Aunt Iris, are you trying to collect Uncle Will's ashes?"

Again she cocked her head, but she didn't answer and didn't look at me.

"The sheriff will give him back when the coroner is finished."

She grimaced.

"Uncle Will was inside the trunk when the car burned. I don't think those are his ashes."

"Go away."

"What are you trying to do?" I persisted.

"Don't tell me what to do!" she snapped, as if she hadn't heard me correctly. "I'm sick to death of listening to voices."

"I'm not one of your voices," I argued. "I'm—"

"I'm not listening! I can't hear you!"

"—Anna."

She dropped the jar and held her hands over her ears. "I can't hear you, I can't hear you, I can't hear you," she chanted loudly.

Seeing that I was upsetting her, I backed away. As I did, she raised her head and looked in my direction.

"Anna? Anna, is that you? Are you dead?" she asked, then answered her own question before I could. "Yes, yes, I can see clearly, you're on the other side now. I shouldn't have let it happen, but I hope you will be happier."

I quickly looked down at my body. I could see through it! It was more like light than substance, and through the sheer light that was me, I saw mud and tire tracks. I stretched out my hand. It was transparent. My God, I *was* dead!

Help me! Uncle Will, help me. I want to go home!

There was a rush of darkness, stars flying past me, as if Uncle Will had caught me with his fishing line and reeled me in through the night. When I opened my eyes, I was lying on my back in bed. I lifted my head to look across the long attic room. What was happening to me?

The Back Door of Midnight

I could move and could see my fingers now, solid skin and bone tightening around the sheet. I was alive. Gradually, my body relaxed. *It was just a nightmare,* I told myself, *like the one I had the night Uncle Will died.* I didn't want to think about why I was having these nightmares. All I wanted to do was stay awake, to keep myself from dreaming again, but my eyes felt tired and gritty, my lids heavy. The weight and weariness of my arms and legs, the humid air, even the damp feel of the sheets—the physical sensation of these things—was reassuring. I gave in and fell asleep.

Six

WHEN I ROLLED over to look at my travel clock the next morning, it was already nine thirty. I sat up quickly, bumping my head on the low ceiling. I listened for a moment, heard nothing but birds, then headed toward the hallway bathroom. Aunt Iris's bedroom door was shut. The image of her sitting in ashy dirt, like a baby plopped down in a sandbox, flashed before my eyes. If the dream hadn't been so weird, I would have laughed. But staying in your uncle's house right after his murder, the same house where your mother was killed, kind of drains the humor from a dream in which your aunt thinks you're dead and says she hopes you will be happier that way.

I put on a pair of capris and a clean top, then organized my backpack. The sheriff was first on my list for that day.

There was no sign of Aunt Iris downstairs. In the kitchen I unplugged and pocketed my cell phone. Hoping to find some cereal and tea, I started opening cupboard doors. I pulled a box of Cheerios from the cabinet above the sink, then stopped, staring at the dish rack below. Sitting among the dried cups and plates was a jar filled with ashes.

I couldn't move—couldn't believe I was seeing it. The birds that had been singing happily a moment ago sounded screechy. The cool air off the creek gave me goose bumps. I gingerly picked up the jar, turning it with the tips of my fingers, then set it down. How had I known about this?

I had never been psychic, and I refused to believe I was becoming that now. If there was such a thing as paranormal ability, then certainly it was a talent you were born with, not a germ spread by contact.

Slow down, think it through, I told myself.

I knew that Iris was upset about not having Uncle Will's remains. I also knew she was crazy. She could have scooped some ashes from somebody's barbecue and convinced herself it was him. As for me, knowing that my aunt was upset and angry, it made sense that I would dream about it.

I had nearly convinced myself of this theory when I noticed Aunt Iris's shoes by the porch door. They were crusted with mud. I turned over the shoes. The ridged soles were covered with ashy earth. I examined my own shoes, speckled with small pieces of grass that had dried on them after last night's walk down to the water, then I ran upstairs to check the slip-ons by my bed and even my sandals still packed in their plastic bag. They were clean. Of course, why would my shoes be crusted like Aunt Iris's, since, in my dream, I didn't have solid feet to wear them? But it didn't make me feel any better that the present situation was consistent with last night's dream.

My search must have awakened Aunt Iris. I heard water running through the noisy pipes in the bathroom. For a moment I considered bolting from the house, driving till I found a Denny's and could think things over with the help of a stack of pancakes. But I got a grip on my imagination and returned to the kitchen.

I was sipping tea and munching dry cereal when Aunt Iris entered the room. She blinked and straightened up, as if she was surprised to see me. *Oh, great,* I thought, *I'm going to have to explain who I am all over again.*

"You're still here," she said.

"Yes. Good morning."

"You're *alive.*"

"I'm Anna," I reminded her.

"I knew that."

"Then why wouldn't I be alive?" I asked.

She shrugged. "I'm not as sure about things as I used to be." She fixed herself tea and sat down at the table.

"Aunt Iris, what's in that jar in the dish rack?"

"William," she said, sounding *quite* sure about that. She reached over and took a handful of dry cereal from my bowl.

"You mean his ashes?"

She nodded and chewed.

"I thought he was at the coroner's."

"I got them from the place where he burned. I went last night."

"Where the car burned," I said.

"It's been towed," she informed me.

"Was anyone else there—last night, I mean?"

"Just the voices."

The skin on the back of my neck crawled. "What did the voices say?"

"Nonsense, all nonsense. I didn't listen."

"And no one else was around?"

She gazed at me, her blue eyes luminous as if lit from behind—*just catching the light from the window,* I told myself.

"I thought you were, but maybe it was Joanna. I thought you were dead, Anna, but here you are alive."

I found myself looking down, checking that my hands weren't transparent.

"Do you want the rest of your cereal?" she asked, dipping her fingers into the bowl for more.

"No, you finish it." I had lost my appetite, watching the

same fingers that had sifted the ashes digging in my Cheerios.

"I'm going into town this morning."

She nodded. "I know, looking for a job. Perhaps, in time, you would like to take on some of my animal clients. The work is getting too much for me."

"Thank you, but I'm not good at that kind of thing."

"In time," she repeated.

I didn't argue. Excusing myself, I hurried upstairs to brush my teeth. I couldn't wait to get back to the normal world.

I walked to town, the bridge being just a quarter of a mile away and the town not much bigger than my neighborhood in Baltimore. Most of Wisteria's streets were tree-lined with brick and clapboard houses, a few dating back to the 1700s, when it was a port and center for commercial fishing. Now it was a college town and summer retreat, with rows of wooden porches and about a zillion flowerpots and hanging baskets. Many of the visitors docked their boats in the marinas along the Sycamore River or stayed at bed-and-breakfasts.

Zack had said the sheriff's office was at the corner of Jib and Water. The one-story brick building looked like a house, except for the municipal flags that were flying outside. A handwritten sign hung on the door: GONE FOR DONUTS.

"Gone for how long?" I exclaimed, exasperated. Turning

on my heel, I ran head-on into a man carrying a paper bag and coffee.

"Sorry . . . Sheriff McManus?"

"That's right."

He was a small man with a sunburned face and short, bristly hair that caught the light like pale velour. He set his coffee and bag on a plastic chair, unlocked the door, and gestured for me to enter.

There was a neat disorder to the room we entered—papers everywhere, but all of them in distinct piles with bricks for paperweights.

"What can I do for you?" he asked, settling into a chair behind a desk. "Have a seat. You're new around here."

"I'm visiting. My name is Anna."

He nodded, opened his bag, and pulled out three packets of sugar, adding all of them to his coffee.

"Anna O'Neill Kirkpatrick."

He had been stirring his coffee. Now he stopped and gazed at me. "Joanna's daughter. Iris's great-niece."

"That's right."

"Last time I saw you, you wore pigtails and ribbons and came up to my elbow. But I don't expect you to remember me. Did Ms. Nolan send you around?"

"Ms. Nolan?"

"Will and Iris's attorney. I've been meaning to ask her if she'd contacted you."

"She didn't."

"Well, then, I'm glad Iris had the sense to call you. I been kinda worried. As far as I know, you're the only other living relative."

"No one called me. Uncle Will wrote to me several weeks back, and I came yesterday, expecting to spend the summer with him."

The sheriff's response was a stare, then a nod. "Must have been a shock. A real shock. Where you living? Was it Baltimore you went to?"

"Yes."

At his request I gave him my home address and phone number, as well as my cell phone number, which he wrote down in a little notebook that he pulled out of his shirt pocket.

"Please tell me everything you know about my uncle's death."

He was silent for a moment, gazing down at his brown bag, then he reached in and asked, "Doughnut?"

"No thanks. I was told some things, but Aunt Iris gets very confused. I'm not sure what to believe. She said he was found in the trunk of a burning car."

"That's right. How old are you, Anna?"

"Almost eighteen. My birthday's in July."

He thought about this, then nodded and said, "The fire department found William in an abandoned car on Tilby's Dream, an old farm on your side of the creek. About fifty percent of his body was burned."

His tone of voice was matter-of-fact—he could have been describing last week's weather—but he was watching me closely, I guess to see how I'd deal with the information. "He was dead before that—how long before, we're waiting to hear. Looks like he died of blunt force trauma to the back of the head, but we'll know more with the coroner's report. We're required to send our bodies to the lab in Baltimore—that's why Iris can't have him back yet. I know she's upset about that."

"She said it happened Wednesday."

"Thursday, actually—after midnight—but we don't yet know when or where he was murdered. Iris said she thought he was off fishing, but she couldn't remember when he had left. She told us that sometimes William went for days. Is that true?"

"I don't know."

"It was William's lawyer, Ms. Nolan, who noticed him missing Monday, the Monday before the fire. William didn't keep a two o'clock appointment, and Ms. Nolan couldn't reach him by phone. Actually, she mentioned this to me at the time, but I wasn't worried, just figured William's mind was going the same winding road as Iris's."

The sheriff turned in his chair and punched a button on a swiveling fan, making the piles of paper rustle from one side of the office to the other, demonstrating his need for a lot of bricks.

"So I'm guessing William died sometime before two o'clock on Monday. Ms. Nolan can't tell me what the appointment was about, but I already know from William that he was petitioning for guardianship of Iris. Did he mention any of this to you?"

"No, sir. What does it mean?"

"He was going to file a request with the courts that he be put in charge of Iris—of everything pretty much—her finances and health care. Basically, the petition says that the other person is incapable of taking care of herself, mentally and otherwise. It's as much power over a person as the law can give, and Iris was fighting it all the way."

That explains her anger, I thought; *she is assuming that Uncle Will secretly invited me to be an ally against her.* And maybe he had.

"Now, I doubt that's any kind of motive for Iris," the sheriff continued, breaking his doughnut in half, dipping an end in his coffee. "If anything, she's psychic, not—" He gave a little shrug.

"Psychotic?" I suggested.

"But I need to figure this out soon as possible," he went on. "I don't want outsiders questioning things—you know, folks who aren't used to Iris and might read into things just because she's a little peculiar.

"Sure you don't want a doughnut?" he asked. "Won't find any better than Jamie's. I get the day-old. Half price, just as good, great with coffee."

"No thanks."

He broke the second cruller in half and dunked. "We searched the house and property and William's boat, which was found empty and adrift a mile or so up the creek. The crime lab's got the boat, looking for stuff the eye can't see, but so far we have no idea where the murder occurred. Do you know of any place your uncle liked to go?"

"No. When I was little, he fished with me off the dock. I didn't go in the boat with him."

"Do you know of any conflicts in his life, any people he didn't get along with?"

Other than Aunt Iris? I thought. "No."

"Maybe you'll think of something and let me know." He looked at me expectantly.

"Zack, from next door, said you were investigating some kids."

"Zack Fleming told you that?"

"Zack Whoever from next door," I replied. "He said there've been three previous arsons, which the police haven't solved."

"And?"

"And that's it. I was hoping you could tell me more."

"Like what?"

"Well, like why you think it was kids."

He nodded. "This site and the others have an amateurish look. And there are always beer bottles, which usually mean high school or college kids partying it up. They like to throw them into the fire."

I flinched. In my first dream an object had whistled close to my ears and exploded, sounding like glass against metal.

"What?" he asked.

"Nothing. It just seems . . . hard to imagine," I said lamely. "Where's Tilby's farm? Can you give me directions?"

"There's nothing much to see there," he said, then tore a sheet from his notebook. "But I guess I'd want a look too."

He drew a map, which I tucked in my pocket.

"William ever talk to you about his relationship with local kids?"

I shook my head. "No. Not really."

He chewed a doughnut and swallowed. "Aside from those 'not really' times, what did he say?"

"Well, he thinks—thought—that most kids today are spoiled, that they're given everything and don't value anything. That's pretty much it."

"Did he ever tell you about someone vandalizing his boat?"

"No."

"Spray painting his truck?"

"No."

"Setting fire to the grass at the top of his driveway?"

"No! I had no idea he was having trouble." I felt badly, as if I should have somehow known and helped him out.

"Are you psychic?" the sheriff asked.

I straightened, surprised. "No."

"Keep your cell phone charged and with you."

Because I couldn't sense danger? Did one statement follow on the other?

"Tell Iris that I'll be coming around to check on how she's doing and that I know she wants William back as soon as possible."

"Okay."

He handed me his card. "Call me. Any thoughts, any questions, any worries. Any time."

"Thanks. There is one other thing. Uncle Will liked to hunt. I went through the house, but I didn't see any guns."

"He kept them locked up in his pickup. Legally, I can't remove them; illegally, I took the key. Do you want it?"

"No. But thanks for doing that."

I asked him for the lawyer's phone number and address,

which he wrote down, then I asked for directions to Jamie's, feeling as if I needed strong coffee and carbohydrates to think through what I had just been told.

"Go for the day-olds," the sheriff advised.

I nodded. "Half price and just as good."

"Exactly." He got a funny look on his face, then laughed. "I told you that."

"Just a few minutes ago."

Seven

ELEVEN A.M., AND it was already hot and humid. I took Water Street over to High, passing a marina, a crab house, and a municipal park, thinking that being close to the river, I'd catch what little breeze there was. High Street, which ended at the river, was Wisteria's "Main Street." On the first block above the intersection with Water were large homes bearing plaques with the words "Historic Landmark." Beyond that block were smaller houses, many of them converted to shops and restaurants.

I found Jamie's place, Tea Leaves Café, on the fourth block up from the water in a long building that had been built as a series of windowed storefronts. After buying six fresh doughnuts and an iced cappuccino, I snagged a seat by the window. It was a comfortable kind of place, with an old tile floor and wooden tables and chairs painted in a rainbow of colors, none of the sets matching. At the back of the café were two cases displaying bakery items, salads, and yogurt. I watched a girl about my age waiting on customers. I wished I were her, working a summer job in a place that seemed friendly—and normal.

Sipping my cappuccino, I gazed out the window at the people walking by, eyeing a family with little kids, suddenly missing Jack, Claire, Grace, and Mom so much that I started to sniffle. I pulled out my cell phone. I could call. I could call and—ruin their vacation? Even if I said everything was fine, my voice might give me away. Instead, I'd text Mom later on and tell her that Wisteria was "interesting."

I dabbed at my nose, then saw a guy standing on the curb across the street, looking in my direction. He was tall, wearing slick sunglasses and a preppy-looking shirt, its sleeves rolled up neatly to the elbows, as if he were working an office job. He smiled a gorgeous smile. I surveyed the sidewalk on my side of the street, then turned to look behind me, wondering who he was smiling at. When I turned back, he pointed in my direction. *You,* he mouthed, and lifted the shades. Zack.

The traffic light changed, and he started across the street, as if he was coming to Tea Leaves. I felt a thump-thump inside my rib cage and realized suddenly that it was my heart. He came through the door and flashed me a grin. Then he joined a girl and guy at a table across the room. *The* girl, the crying girl, the hot costar.

I don't know why I hadn't noticed her—I was probably

ogling the baked goods—for she was straight out of Drama Club at my old school, the kind of person who was on stage even when she wasn't. A table of tweens watched her with awe as she talked with Zack and the other guy. The other guy had brown hair streaked with peroxide and close-set eyes with brows rising toward the center. A smile would have made him cute in a quirky way, but his mouth was a long straight line.

Pulling my eyes away from the three of them, I got out my map of the town and the sheriff's map to the burn site, trying to focus on what I was here to do. I'd call the lawyer, find a food store, look for—

"Hi, Anna."

I glanced up. "Hi . . . hi."

"Zack," he said, as if I might have forgotten his name.

I nodded. "Zack Fleming."

He smiled, not only with his mouth, but with his amazing eyes.

"The sheriff told me your last name."

That got rid of the smile.

"Saving this seat for anyone?" He assumed I wasn't and sat down.

"So . . . so you spoke to him," said Zack.

"Just now."

"Was he helpful?"

"In what way?"

Zack hesitated. "In whatever way you need help."

There was something about the tone of his voice. He was worried.

"Yes and no."

He waited for me to say more. His friends at the other table were watching us closely.

He tried again. "Have the police learned anything new?"

"I doubt it."

"So what did McManus say?" he persisted.

"Nothing much more than you did."

Two can play this game, I thought. I didn't trust him. Worse, I didn't trust myself not to be suckered in by those deep-as-a-quarry, understanding eyes. I looked out the window.

When I glanced back, he was eyeing the maps I had spread in front of me. "What are you looking for?" he asked.

I shrugged and studied High Street again. "A lot of things. A grocery store, a muffler shop, my aunt's lawyer, a murderer."

His hand rested on mine. "That's a big list," he said gently.

I pulled my hand away. "Yes."

"It must be really hard for you."

I looked him in the eye. "Not as hard as it is for Aunt Iris. And not half as hard as it was for an old man whose property was being vandalized by spoiled kids."

Zack sat back in his chair. There was a guarded expression on his face.

A quick glance told me the girl and guy at the other table were still watching us intently. "Do your friends lip-read?" I asked.

Zack turned, then nodded at them. I didn't know what that gesture meant. Maybe he was telling his friends *yes* in response to some question they'd asked; maybe he was just acknowledging the fact that they were staring at us. Turning to me again, he said, "I've got to get back to work," then rose and left the café.

I shrugged off his abruptness. When he was gone, I gathered up my stuff and walked toward the small waterside park I had passed earlier. I found a bench close to the river and put in a call to the lawyer's office. Her secretary gave me an appointment for three that afternoon, plus directions to a food store and a local gas station, one that would fix mufflers. I was feeling better now, more in control, working down my list of things to do. For a moment I relaxed, gazing out at the river, listening to the clink-clink of a line against the mast of an anchored boat. I watched a sailboat tack, its triangle of white shifting, becoming dazzling against the blue.

Suddenly, I had the feeling that someone was watching me. I turned around.

He was sprawled under a tree, the guy I had seen at Tea

Leaves, the one sitting with Zack's girlfriend. I turned back to the river. *It's a park,* I reminded myself; *people come here to sit and gaze at the river.* But I felt uneasy. I couldn't shake the feeling he was here because I was.

I exited the park, acting as if I hadn't noticed him. As I walked up High Street, I glanced once over my shoulder, but I didn't see him, not till I doubled back to check what was playing at the movie theater. He slowed to a stop and found something interesting in a store window.

I moved on. He moved on. I crossed the street. He crossed the street. Did he think I wouldn't notice him, or did he hope I would? Maybe this was harassment; after all, he knew I could identify him as Zack's friend. This was just a game.

Game or not, I was getting ticked. I longed to confront him, but city living had taught me that you don't confront people you don't know. I darted up a set of steps and into a shop. If he followed me into a place with a shopkeeper and some kind of security, then I'd take him on.

Looking down from the shop window, I saw him stop in the middle of the brick sidewalk. His long, thin mouth shaped itself into a smile, as if he were amused by the fact that his rabbit had found a hole. He glanced up. At first I thought he saw me, but he was looking higher, at the words painted on the window. It took me a moment to decode the backward letters:

ALWAYS CHRISTMAS. It was easy, however, to read his response: the F word. I wondered why his amusement would change so quickly to anger. He moved on. I hoped he was giving up, not waiting out of sight.

"May I help you?"

I turned quickly, then stepped away from catastrophe: One swing of my backpack and I would have cleared a shelf of ceramic angels.

"Is there something I can help you with?" the woman asked, eyeing my backpack.

"This is a nice shop." My response sounded lame.

"Thank you."

I needed to buy some time, to encourage Zack's friend to find another quarry.

"May I look around?"

"I'm not open for business on Mondays, but *if* you are careful, I see no harm."

"I think I'll put my backpack by the door."

"Good idea."

I had been in Christmas shops at Jersey and Maryland beaches, but boardwalk stores can be a little junky and usually smell like seawater and tar. In this shop aggressive air-conditioning made it as dry as winter; spicy smells gave it a holiday mood. The walls were painted in midnight blue, and carefully placed spotlights made snowflakes sparkle. Figu-rines painted in old-fashioned clothes and antique-looking angels perched and dangled everywhere. The shop created a once-upon-a-time Christmas—the kind everyone likes to "remember," even though most of us haven't experienced it. I looked at things I would never buy—not with those price tags—working my way around the store until I reached the cash register.

HELP WANTED, the sign said, and in small print, MINIMUM 3 YRS. RETAIL EXPERIENCE. I wondered if wrapping up bagels and sandwiches would be considered retail. It didn't matter—I just wanted to use up time.

"I'd like to apply for the job."

The woman looked up, surprised. "I require at least three years' retail experience."

"Are you the owner?"

The woman smiled a little. She had a sleek brown bob and light eyes accentuated by expert makeup. "I am."

"I'd like to apply. Is there a form to fill out?"

She flipped open a book and pulled out an application form. I took my time filling it out, using Aunt Iris's address and phone number, then handed it back.

She read the name and address and glanced up. "I should have known by the hair. You're an O'Neill."

"Yes."

She held out her hand. "I'm Marcy Fleming."

Fleming. "Zack's mother?"

That's why the stalker hadn't liked my rabbit hole. He thought I was running straight to Zack's mom—stepmom.

"Stepmother," she corrected, then smiled. "I owe you for yesterday. Thank you for getting rid of our four-legged friends."

I nodded.

"How is Iris doing?" she asked.

"I—I'm not sure. There are a lot of things I have to figure out. She's not really—uh—"

"Normal? Then I guess she is doing the same as before. It was very decent of you to come," Mrs. Fleming added. "There aren't a lot of young people who would visit their batty aunt."

"I didn't come for that reason." It seemed as if I had given this spiel a hundred times since arriving. "Uncle Will invited me. He said there were some family things to talk about, so I came expecting to see him."

"You mean you didn't know? Oh, I'm sorry! I'm so sorry. Someone should have informed you."

"According to Aunt Iris, *Uncle Will* should have."

She smiled a little. "How long will you be staying?"

"I don't know yet. I have college orientation in August."

"So you're looking for a summer job."

What could I say? No, I'm as paranoid as Aunt Iris and think people are following me. . . .

"Yes, but the truth is, I don't have the experience you want. I worked at Panera Bread for two years—you know, handling bagels, sandwiches, that kind of thing."

"I see. And how many bagels a week would you say you dropped?"

"I had a counter in front of me. There was no place to drop them."

She laughed a tinkly laugh that seemed too girlish to go with her businesslike appearance. "You're hired."

"Excuse me?"

"Honesty is important. And I need an employee who knows how to position herself so she doesn't drop things. Of course," she added, "Zack would advise you not to take this job."

"Why?" I asked bluntly.

That tinkly laugh again. "I'm a tough stepmother and a tough employer. Sometimes we're swamped, other times it's slow. When it is, I'll expect you to help with cleaning, inventory, whatever I need. There is no slacking off in my shop. And there is certainly no socializing, no little visits from friends."

I thought fast. Aunt Iris's problems weren't going to be solved in a week, probably not in several weeks.

"What were you paid at Panera?"

I told her.

"I can match that. And on the bright side," she went on, "I would understand if you have an emergency involving Iris and couldn't come to work. I also know you will be leaving for school. You realize, of course, no one in town will hire you if they think you are leaving in August. But some help now will get me through the longest days of the tourist season."

Working in a shop might keep me sane; it would definitely keep me in air-conditioning. It would give me extra money for college—and a new muffler. The only strange thing was Mrs. Fleming's connection to Zack. But I liked her. She was no-nonsense and blunt, the kind of person I found easy to get along with.

"I'm thinking ten to five Wednesday through Saturday, twelve to five on Sunday." She cocked her head. "Interested?"

"Yes."

"When can you start?"

"Wednesday."

"Training tomorrow," she said.

"Okay."

She folded her arms and appeared pleased. "It will be worth your time, Anna. If you do the job well, I'll teach you more than clerking a store. You'll learn how to run your own business."

"Awesome."

"There's a small lot in the back for parking. Don't block me in. See you tomorrow."

A few minutes later I was hurrying home to Aunt Iris's. Zack's friend must have given up the game. Aunt Iris was out, so I got to enjoy the rest of my doughnuts on the kitchen stoop, gazing at the creek. At noon I roared off to the gas station to get a new muffler, then drove more quietly to Tilby's Dream.

The old farm lay along Oyster Creek on the eastern bank, like the O'Neill house, but on the other side of Scarborough Road, past the bridge. "Can't miss it," the sheriff had told me. "Got a big old tulip poplar on the corner"—whatever a tulip poplar was. I drove slowly, looking at every large tree I passed—there were a lot—and finally turned onto the first paved road I saw.

McManus had said to go almost to the end, then turn right on an unmarked dirt road, hidden by trees. Mrs. Fleming—Marcy, as I was supposed to call her—had looked at my penciled map and said the road was used for hayrides in the fall, but she couldn't remember any kind of landmark helpful for a girl like me who was used to road signs and marked intersections. I drove more than a mile through golden green fields of soy and corn, then spotted a grove of trees that might be camouflaging a dirt road. Since I had been warned about potholes, I pulled over and got out to walk.

I knew I was in the right place when I saw the deep tracks made by heavy equipment that had passed through recently—fire trucks, I assumed. The trees that lined both sides of the road had been planted at even intervals, perhaps to make a shady avenue, but were now overgrown with shrubs, vines, and smaller trees. Although it wasn't wilderness, to a city person it was the middle of nowhere. There wasn't even the distant whoosh of traffic that afternoon, the cornfields and trees shielding the road from every sound but that of insects.

After ten minutes of walking, I reached the site. In my dreams I had come in darkness; now the site was bathed in sunlight, but the smell was the same—pine and sour ashes. It was unnerving to feel that a place was very familiar when I had never physically set foot on it.

I surveyed the area surrounded by yellow police tape. The scorched ground was sandy with pieces of shell embedded in it, oyster shells, like those on Aunt Iris's driveway. Perhaps there had been a building here once. On either side of the clearing were fields. The one on the right was nothing but dried stalks and was hemmed with a stand of pine; the one on the left stretched to distant woods with row after row of green soy.

The dirt road continued past the burn site and through

another avenue of trees. I recalled the sounds of sirens and running feet from my first dream. If fire trucks had entered from one direction, it would have been easy for the kids setting the blaze to exit through the other. It seemed an ideal place for arson.

I ducked under the police tape and walked to the center of the cordoned-off area. Standing there, I turned slowly, my eyes sweeping the landscape. It was like looking at something in a wavy mirror, like looking at your living room reflected in a Christmas ball, finding it both strange and familiar. Somehow, the image of this place had gotten inside my head. Somehow, it had rooted in my brain before I had seen the place for real, and it scared me.

Eight

WHEN I ARRIVED home at dinnertime, Aunt Iris was sitting at the kitchen table making a sandwich. "You're back," she said, sounding surprised.

I was about to explain who I was and why I was here, then decided it wasn't worth the trouble, as long as she thought I was myself or my mother. "I got a job, Aunt Iris. And I've been to the grocery store."

"We have plenty of food," she replied.

I eyed the two pieces of slimy meat she had just laid on her bread and the mayo jar with yellow, crusty stuff inside the rim. "Thanks, but I don't want to be mooching off of you. I bought one of those already-cooked rotisserie chickens. Want to try it?"

Without waiting for her response, I slid her sandwich plate to the side and placed the plastic container with chicken in front of her. She studied it for a moment, then picked up the butcher knife she'd been using and hacked off a leg.

"Where will you be working, Anna?"

So she did know who I was. "At a store called Always Christmas."

"Marcy's shop. That's very nice."

She sounded normal, making me wonder if she had taken some kind of medicine. I thought it took longer for psychiatric drugs to work.

"I hope you remembered to get Dr Pepper," she said, watching me put away groceries.

"I did. Want some?"

"No, thank you," Aunt Iris replied. "I have private matters to attend to."

I opened the refrigerator and moved to one side all the stuff I planned to throw out when she wasn't looking.

"It's unfortunate," she said.

"What is?" I asked, wiping off the cleared shelf with a dishrag.

"I really can't say. They are private matters."

"All right."

"I'll be in my office."

I pulled my head out of the refrigerator in time to see her slip a key into the door that led from the kitchen into the next room, the one I'd found locked last night. Curious, I followed her to the door to see what was there.

Two of the room's walls had glass-fronted cabinets with counters beneath, the kind you see in an old science lab. There was a desk, what looked like an examining table, and an old-fashioned scale. A bookshelf just inside the door was crammed with worn volumes on the care of horses, cows, sheep, and, yes, goats.

"Was this my great-grandfather's office?" I asked.

Aunt Iris swung around. "I told you some things are private!"

"Okay, okay," I said, taking a step back.

She sat down at the desk, which was topped with a collection of candleholders, all of them covered with wax, their candles burnt down to the metal. What did she do in here?

"Don't," she said.

"Don't what?"

"I can hear you prying. It's nobody's fault."

"It isn't?" I replied, not sure what she was talking about.

"Of course not," she said. "People just die."

"Sooner or later."

"On your way out, Joanna, close the door behind you."

Obviously, I was supposed to leave. I returned to the kitchen but kept the door cracked between us. A minute later she closed and locked it—I heard the double click. Oh, *well*.

I fixed myself a salad and ate the other chicken leg,

listening for movement inside her office, hearing nothing. Thinking about the melted candles, I sniffed but couldn't smell anything burning. While she was occupied with "private matters," I cleared the gross stuff out of the fridge, triple bagging it, then took it out to a set of heavy-duty trash cans next to Uncle Will's pickup. On my way back to the kitchen I saw that Iris had closed the shutters in her office.

Once inside again, I called to her. "Aunt Iris?"

She didn't respond.

"Aunt Iris, can I help you with anything?"

"No, these are private matters."

Tomorrow I was buying several smoke detectors. "All right. I'm going down to the dock for a while."

Sitting on the dock, I turned my back to the house, but I couldn't shut her out of my mind. According to her lawyer, there were a lot of decisions to be made. Turning eighteen in a month and being the one-and-only "next of kin" to Aunt Iris, I would have to make choices that were far beyond my own experience. Ms. Nolan had strongly suggested that I call Mom. I would, but after her vacation. Tomorrow's text message would be "GETTING 2 KNO AUNT IRIS + LUV THE CREEK."

Lost in thought, I didn't notice the steady sound of flicking water coming from the left, not until cool drops were flicked at me.

"Earth to Anna," Zack called.

I turned and saw him treading water about eight feet from the dock. His wet hair was slicked straight back and dripped down his neck, almost touching his shoulders. Some people look weird wet and slick, but not Zack.

"Hi."

"Hi! Come on in," he invited. "Water's great."

"Looks great, but no thanks."

"Come on," he coaxed.

"I'm not wearing a bathing suit."

"So?"

"So," I said firmly.

"Do you like boats? I've got a rowboat." He pulled a tan arm out of the water to gesture in the direction of the Flemings' dock. "Want to use it?"

I had always wanted to take out a boat—I mean a real one, not the purple sea dragons that I had pedaled in the Baltimore harbor. Floating around on an evening like this . . .

"I'll row for you."

"I can row myself," I said—not that I ever had.

"Okay. There's a gate through the hedge, close to the house."

I glanced in the direction of the Flemings' dock, then back at the gate.

"Meet you over there," he said, and swam toward his own dock.

Well, how hard can rowing be? I asked myself as I crossed from one yard to the other. It was a children's song—*Row, row, row your boat.* But when I walked out on the Flemings' dock, I had second thoughts. There was an expensive-looking cabin cruiser tied next to the rowboat, and I imagined myself rowing into it. These things didn't have brakes.

Zack was floating on his back. When he saw me looking at the cabin cruiser, he righted himself. "Do you like big boats? Our sailboat's at the marina. We can't get its mast under the bridge."

And where do you keep your oceangoing yacht? I felt like asking. I stared down at the water. I didn't remember the boats in Baltimore's harbor sitting that many feet below the dock.

Zack swam closer. "Want some help getting in? Tide's low."

"I can manage it," I assured him, and jumped. I landed squarely on both feet, the force of my leap making the boat rock wildly. I rocked with it and grabbed the piling to which the boat was tied, holding on to it like a cat clinging to a tree.

When I peeked at Zack, he had ducked under the water. From the bubbles coming up, I knew he was laughing.

"Next time," he said, when he'd surfaced, "you might want to sit on the dock and ease yourself down to the boat."

"I might."

"Why don't you put on the life jacket," he suggested, "just in case the coast guard comes by."

The coast guard wasn't coming by; Zack thought I needed something to keep me afloat, and he was probably right.

I let go of the piling, sat down, and pulled on the clumsy padding. Slipping the oars in the oarlocks—that was surprisingly easy to figure out—I was about to shove off when, just in time, I remembered I was still tied to the piling. Now, that would have been embarrassing.

I quickly leaned forward and untied the rope, trying to look as if I knew what I was doing. When the difficult knot finally came undone, I noticed Zack once again making like a submarine, sending up flurries of bubbles. I bit my lip.

He surfaced choking. I pretended not to notice.

"You know," he said, "if there is only one rope, it works better to free the loop attached to the dock. That way, if you dock somewhere else, you will still have a rope in the boat."

I glanced at the rope, which dangled forlornly from the dock. "Fortunately, as it turns out, I will be coming back here."

He grinned. "Fortunately."

I pushed off from the piling, letting the boat float itself away from the dock and cabin cruiser, then picked up the oars and started rowing. It wasn't as easy as I had thought. Sometimes I lowered the oars too deeply and could barely drag them out of the water; other times I skipped them along the surface, dousing myself. My right arm was stronger than my left, which meant I rowed in circles. Since I had already proven I didn't know what I was doing, there was no point in worrying about how I looked to Zack. I kept rowing. I rowed till my shoulders and arms ached, determined to master the skill.

Zack left me alone, watching me from time to time but saying nothing as he swam around and floated on his back. Perhaps he read my body language and knew I wouldn't welcome his help.

Finally, with the skin on my hands rubbed raw, I had to stop. I floated about, watching how the sun melted in a pool behind the bridge, leaving the western sky a fiery pink, enjoying the sounds—the voices and laughter that carried across from the other side of the creek. The floor of the boat was gritty. I brushed off a spot and lowered myself onto it, resting my back against one of the two seat slats, cushioning my spine with the life vest. I could have floated out there all night, watching the sky fade to lilac.

"Hello!" Zack had popped up like a smiling porpoise and was hanging on to the bow of the boat, his arms and shoulders resting along the boat's edge. "Permission to board, Captain?"

Without waiting for an answer, he heaved himself over the side of the boat—wet, muscular shoulders and arms, powerful legs. I stared at him, pulling myself up onto the boat seat. *Stop looking at him,* I told myself. But it was hard not to, since he took up most of the space in front of me.

"Switch places," he said. "Take it slowly, Anna, okay?"

"Sure." For a moment we had a slow dance in the middle of the boat, he steadying me with his wet hands and laughing when I bolted for the other seat. "You're determined to sink this thing!"

He sat down in the rower's seat and picked up the oars. "I thought you might like a tour of our neck of the creek. A quick one, before it gets dark," he said, glancing at the sky.

His eyes were the color of the sky at twilight. There was a soft light in them, like the last bit at the end of the day. As he rowed across the creek, I forced myself to look at the shoreline rather than him.

"That's a little park," he said, pausing a moment to point, "used mostly by people from Chase College. The campus is back in that direction. The pavilion belongs to them, but everybody uses it to picnic. Those docks are for their crew and sailing teams."

Beyond the college waterfront we passed a large house with terraced gardens, then crossed over the creek to glide by another estate. Estates, crew teams, a guy rowing me around—I felt as if I had slipped between the pages of a British novel.

"That's the Fairfaxes' place."

"I can see the roof above the trees. That's a lot of roof!"

"The house is large," he said, as if he didn't live in a manse.

"There's no dock," I observed.

"They like their privacy. You can't see it well in this light, but they let the lower part of their grounds on each side go wild and marshy, so you can't walk—you can't even wade the shoreline all the way through. They own several houses and are here only in the fall and spring. They put out a floating dock then. It's Marcy's family," he said. "Her adoptive family."

"Her *adoptive* family?" He had hit a nerve. "Meaning not her real family?"

"Sorry?"

"Meaning just her adoptive family, which is something less than being her birth family?"

He frowned. "I didn't mean that at all."

"Then why even mention it?" I asked. *Let it go, Anna,* I told myself, but I couldn't.

"Because Marcy mentions it—a lot." He had stopped rowing and was studying my face, as if trying to understand. "You're adopted," he guessed.

"Obviously."

"Your family must miss you," he said.

If he thought I was going to give him the details of my family life, he was wrong. We floated in silence.

"You said they were on vacation. Where?"

"Massachusetts."

"So, do you have any brothers and sisters?" Halfway through the question, he hesitated, as if he thought I might jump down his throat again.

"Two sisters and a brother." The boat rocked gently, the water lapping against its side. "How about you?"

He shook his head. "Just Dad. And Marcy."

"I like Marcy," I said.

He looked surprised. "You do? You've met her?"

"I'm working for her."

"You're *what*?!"

"She hired me today."

He grimaced. "Well, good luck."

"I'm surprised your friend didn't tell you that I stopped by her shop." The tone of my voice gave away my feelings about his friend.

"What friend?" he asked, caution seeping into his voice.

"The guy at Tea Leaves. The guy who followed me down to the park, then up High Street. Either he's a lousy stalker or he was trying to intimidate me."

Without comment, Zack picked up the oars and started to row.

"Why?" I asked. "Why did he do that?"

Zack's face was a mask, his eyes avoiding mine, which was a mistake: As long as I wasn't looking in his eyes, I had a fighting chance against the spell they cast.

"What is your friend's connection to the fire?" I persisted. "What is his connection to my uncle's death? What's yours?"

He rowed in silence. We rounded a bend in the creek, and his home slid into view.

"Tell me what you know," I demanded.

"It's complicated, Anna."

"There's nothing like facts to make things simpler."

But he wouldn't answer me. Letting one oar drop, he steered with the other as we drifted toward the Flemings' dock. His long fingers caught the rope that I had so carefully untied. While he secured the boat, I unfastened my life jacket.

"You have three choices," Zack said. "You can climb without my help and scrape your knees. I can give you a push from behind. Or I can climb out first and give you a hand from above. Which would you like?"

"A hand from above."

He scrambled out of the boat, then extended his hand, pulling me up easily.

"Anna." He stood so close, I could smell the creek on him. "Take care of Iris. And let the police take care of the rest."

Mere closeness was as dangerous as his eyes. "Is that advice or a warning?" I asked.

"Both."

Nine

I WALKED TOWARD the gate in the hedge alone, veering from Zack's path as soon as I could. I heard a dog barking, a shrill whistle, then the sound of a door closing. The yard was suddenly quiet.

"I've been waiting for you."

The voice came from behind me, and I jumped, letting go of the gate I had just opened.

"I didn't mean to scare you," the woman said. The voice was that of an older woman. In the thin light coming from the Flemings' windows, her hair looked white, a fluffy halo around her head. "You're Joanna's daughter."

"Yes. I'm Anna."

"I saw you with the goats yesterday."

I remembered the stocky figure in the black-and-white uniform. "And I saw you," I told her. "Do you work for the Flemings?"

"My name is Audrey Sanchez."

She said it as if that should mean something to me. It didn't. "Nice to meet you."

"Are you psychic, Miss O'Neill?"

"My last name is Kirkpatrick now," I said, but smiled, relieved to know that something as silly as that was on her mind. "And no, I'm not. The farmer refused to leave until he got some advice, so I pretended to do what Aunt Iris does."

"What Iris does is wrong."

"Excuse me?"

"It is an unnatural ability," the woman said. "Iris's knowledge is unholy. It is against God's laws. Her ways are the ways of the devil."

For a moment I wasn't sure what to say. "Well . . . well, everyone is entitled to an opinion, and I suppose that's yours."

"And God's," she replied.

"You talk to him directly?"

"Every day."

"In prayer," I said, hoping that was all she meant. If she imagined it was by Verizon, Aunt Iris wasn't the only loony on Oyster Creek.

"I can tell you are an innocent girl," Ms. Sanchez said, "and that concerns me. You need to be careful." There was genuine worry in her voice. "This is a house of evil."

"Oh!"

"It is so easy to stray." One doughy hand massaged the other as she spoke. "William strayed."

"Uncle Will?"

"He was once righteous and God-fearing, but he turned toward the darkness."

"Really."

"If he hadn't, he would not have suffered a fiery death."

I stared at her. "What do you mean?"

"Psychics are the tools of the devil. Perhaps you weren't aware of it, but William protected Iris. He was in league with her and therefore brought on his own death. It was the only thing that could save him—fire here rather than fire hereafter."

By that, I assumed she meant hell. "I see. Well, thanks for the advice. I'm getting a lot of it tonight." I pushed open the gate, but the woman caught it, pulling it closed.

"What was Iris burying today?"

I faced her. "When?"

"About ten o'clock this morning."

Right after I went out.

"She had a jar," the woman went on.

"Oh, that. Uncle Will's ashes—at least she thinks they are. Where did she put them?"

"Behind the old kitchen."

Close to Uncle Will's den. That made sense.

"Be careful, girl," Ms. Sanchez warned. "Evil draws evil. If something tells you to get out of the house, get out."

"Don't worry," I replied, "I don't usually argue with voices."

Her eyebrows drew together. "Are you hearing them?"

"Not yet."

She touched my arm lightly. "I am here if you need my help."

Just what I needed, another crazy lady. "Thanks. G'night."

On the back step of the House of Evil, I enjoyed an icy glass of Dr Pepper, then went in and took a shower undisturbed. I called good night to Aunt Iris, who wished me the same from the other side of her bedroom door. Not only did she remember I was Anna, she had thoughtfully set a fan on the bureau by my bed. With a day's worth of heat trapped beneath the roof, I turned it on full blast and aimed it at my bed, where I lay down, thinking I'd never fall asleep. Less than five minutes later, I closed my eyes.

I awoke to a low vibrating sound. At first I thought it was the fan, but the sound grew louder, more intense. Remembering my previous dreams, I waited anxiously for what came next. The strange electrical buzz ran through my body, making each nerve ending tingle. I tried to raise my arms and found them as useless as dead things. I couldn't even blink my eyes.

Let go, I told myself, recalling the words that had released me once before from the noise and paralysis. *Let go,* I repeated in my head over and over, until not only my mind but my heart gave up the struggle against something that seemed meant to be.

For a moment all I knew was darkness, then, at the top of the blackness, I saw a silvery outline, the wall like that of a castle. Immediately, I found the door in the wall and went through it. The maze of paths was there, just as before, and the tall figures, blurred forms. I remembered that during my last dream experience, when I had complained to Aunt Iris about my vision, it had cleared a little.

"Aunt Iris, I can't see. I want to see what that is."

I found myself gazing at a rabbit. Tall as a person, its posture was almost human, like that of an animal character in a children's book. I ventured closer, wanting to see what its rough surface was made of, when suddenly, I began to fall—Alice down the rabbit hole!

When the falling stopped, I knew where I was: the burn site. I heard someone behind me and turned quickly. The scene swam in my head, the images colliding, wobbling, then settling.

A girl had run past me. A guy was chasing her. Zack.

He didn't appear to see me, having eyes only for the girl he had just caught in his arms, the girl who was at Tea Leaves, the girl at his stepmother's party.

"Erika, stop! This is crazy!" He pulled her back against him.

She slumped over the arm he had around her, and for a moment I thought she was hurt, then she straightened up and let him turn her so that she faced him, his big hands handling her gently. I thought she would see me as Aunt Iris had, but she didn't.

"I'm afraid," she said to Zack, tears running down her face. "I'm really afraid."

"We'll figure this out," he replied, his voice soft and low.

"Just being here gives me an eerie feeling."

"Then why do you keep coming back?" he asked.

Good question, buddy. Obviously, I didn't buy the tears.

"I've got to find my cell phone. I must have dropped it along the path."

"I told you, Erika, if any evidence was left behind, the police already have it."

"I feel like someone is watching us. I feel it, Zack." She pressed her face into his shoulder.

Why do guys fall for this stuff? I thought.

"You're imagining things." He stroked her hair as if he were soothing a child.

I wanted to flap my arms like a ghost and howl at her. Actually, I did, but she hadn't a clue I was standing there.

"But what if there *is* something to this psychic thing?" Erika asked Zack. "What if the old lady knows?"

"Iris is confused," Zack replied. "I've heard people say she's been crazy for years. Even if she does know something, nothing she says will be believed by the police."

"She scares me."

Zack shook his head. "I told you before—"

"That you were here for me," Erika said. "Are you still?"

"I don't turn my back on friends."

"Then I'm counting on you to keep her niece busy."

Zack was silent for a moment. "I'm not sure I know what you mean."

"Date her."

"What?"

"Hang out with her. Pretend you're interested." She laughed lightly. "Pretend you think she's the most beautiful girl in the world."

"I don't think that's a good idea."

"Why not?" Erika asked. "You told me you don't want to get hooked up with any one girl, not with college ahead. You don't want commitments, and all that crap. Well, let the freckled little carrot be your bodyguard. Hang out with her."

"You're assuming she'd want to hang out with me," he said.

"Oh, puh-lease! There isn't a girl on this planet who wouldn't, and you know it! Go ahead, give her a thrill, and help me out at the same time."

"There are better ways to get information," Zack argued.

"There is no better way to keep tabs on Iris," she replied. "What's the problem? Is Anna that bad? You can't fake it with her?"

"I can fake it with anyone."

"Then do it, okay? Please. For me? Zack, they could nail me with the old man's death."

"That's impossible."

"Then with arson. Arson doesn't look good to a college admission board."

"I'll think about it," he said.

You do that, I thought. *You see if you can fake it with the freckled little carrot.*

Obviously, my feelings were hurt. I felt like a fool for letting down my guard, for looking in his eyes, for admiring his shoulders, for enjoying the way he stood close to me on the dock. *Why do girls fall for this stuff?* I thought.

I want to go back! I want to be asleep, having normal dreams like a normal person. I want out of here!

As before, wanting it badly enough seemed to make it happen. There was a rush of darkness, that same sensation of being reeled back. When I opened my eyes, I was lying in bed, staring at the low ceiling, feeling the breeze of the old fan.

I pulled myself up on one elbow to look at my clock:

The Back Door of Midnight

12:30 a.m. I lay back down, hoping it had been nothing more than a weird dream, but believing otherwise. Last time, the morning after, I had found Aunt Iris's jar of ashes. What would it be this time? I was exhausted from all that was going on and should have been sleeping soundly in this dark and quiet house. Why did some part of me keep slipping out the back door of midnight?

Ten

THE NEXT MORNING I arrived at Always Christmas at the same time as Marcy. The shop was stuffy and silent when we entered through the back door, but within twenty minutes, the AC had kicked in, potpourri was spicing the air, and carols were playing. My odd summer night seemed far away.

For the next several hours I ran the cash register, learned the basics of the shop's computer software, checked out the cleaning supplies, and wiped down the bathroom sink. During my "free" moments, I was expected to study the merchandise, memorizing the names and styles of artists who supplied the shop.

Marcy waited on customers and introduced me by my first name to two people who were local. I was grateful to her for not mentioning that I was an O'Neill.

Late in the afternoon a craftsman who supplied her store, a man who made strange little elves—carved and painted figures that looked a lot like himself—studied me as I studied his work.

"How's things in the neighborhood?" he asked Marcy, still eyeing me.

"Fine."

"How's Iris? Behaving herself?"

"I haven't seen her recently," Marcy replied. "The tourist season keeps me busy."

"That was bad news, finding Will in a trunk. Can't say I'm surprised."

"I'm sure it has been very hard for her. So, have you reduced the price on these elves?"

But the man wasn't going to be sidestepped. "You're an O'Neill," he said to me.

Denying it would have been an insult to my birth family. "Yes."

"Her niece—no, great-niece."

I nodded.

"Are you psychic?"

"No, sir. Psychotic."

The man raised his eyebrows, then laughed. All the little elves on the countertop appeared to laugh with him.

Marcy remained focused on business, examining the figures, turning each one in her hands. "This one is flawed," she said, setting it aside.

"So why did Iris kill William?" the man asked.

"Excuse me?"

"Why did she kill him?"

It was the eyes, I decided, the bulging little eyeballs and the mouth that smiled with cleverness rather than happiness that made the elves look like him.

"That's what everyone is saying, that Iris did it," the man went on. "Some friends of mine take their cats to Iris, and they say she's—" He made the motion for crazy, winding his bony index finger around his ear. "They say she's hearing voices these days."

"It seems to me," I replied, "that the kind of people who take their cats to a psychic should expect her to hear voices."

"But these are different voices," he insisted. "Wicked ones, according to her. She yells at the voices and tells them she won't listen anymore."

I couldn't argue that point, having witnessed her doing it. Still, I felt protective toward her. "If hearing voices and getting confused make you a murderer, retirement homes would be dangerous places." I turned to Marcy. "Is this a good time to finish unpacking the boxes in the back?"

She nodded. "I'll call if I need you."

Ten minutes later, when the artist had left, I returned to the front of the store. "I know I should apologize for being rude, especially to someone as important as a supplier. The problem is, *he* was rude, and I don't feel very sorry."

"I don't blame you," said Marcy. "I don't know why people jump on Iris. I suppose they fear what they don't understand."

"I'm a little afraid of her," I admitted, "but with Uncle Will gone, somebody has to help."

"She's a lot to handle. Isn't there another family member who can share the burden? There has to be a cousin somewhere."

I shook my head. "Neither she nor Uncle Will had children. My birth mother was their only niece, and I'm my mother's only child."

"Where is your adoptive mother?"

"In Massachusetts with my younger brother and sisters. I don't want to interrupt Mom's vacation. We didn't take one last year, and she'll have the kids all by herself when I go to college. She needs a break. I can handle this."

Marcy studied me as carefully as she did the little elves, but rather than discarding me as flawed, she smiled. "I knew I hired the right girl."

That evening I planned to check out the "burial plot" behind Uncle Will's den and begin a careful search of his office for anything that might be helpful for me to know. Finding the makeshift grave wasn't hard. An old shovel had been left propped against the wall, close to an area of soft, upturned earth. The sandy dirt had a black handle sticking out of it, which I pulled: a butcher knife.

A long, sharp knife wasn't what I would have chosen to mark a place where I wanted someone to rest in peace. On the other hand, the site wasn't far from the kitchen and a knife would slide into the earth easily. So which was it, convenience or symbolism? And was anything other than a jar of cinders buried here?

I glanced toward the window of Aunt Iris's office. She had said she'd be working there tonight, so this probably wasn't a good time to dig up Uncle Will. And if she heard me searching his den, the room next to hers, she'd accuse me of scheming with his ghost to get rid of her. I put back the knife. My tasks would have to wait.

Heading toward the water, I heard a jingling of metal tags. The gate between the Flemings' house and ours had been left ajar. A dog pushed his nose through, then came bounding toward me, ears flying, tail bobbing. He looked like a beagle, a very friendly one—my knees and then my chin got a good washing.

Kneeling in the grass, I reached for his tag. HI. I'M CLYDE, it said, and gave a phone number.

"Hello, Clyde."

He sniffed me all over, then gave me a kiss on the ear.

A shrill whistle split the air. "Clyde!"

I looked toward the gate. "Your master calls."

But Clyde wasn't all that obedient. He wagged his tail at me as if to say, *Ignore him. I want to play with you.*

I heard Zack call again.

"Come on, buddy." I walked the dog back to the gate.

Zack was sitting on the patio—or maybe, when a flagstone area is bigger than my backyard at home, has glass-topped tables, black iron chairs, lanterns, and footed urns of flowers, you are supposed to call it a "terrace." Anyway, he was sitting there with a spiral pad open on his lap. When he saw me, he smiled. "Good dog! *Nice fetch!*"

"He wasn't fetching."

"Bring her here, boy. Good job!"

The dog looked from Zack to me.

"I've been training him," Zack said. "Up till now he's brought home only dead rabbits, but I guess he's finally getting the hang of it."

"Great." I turned my back to leave.

Zack jumped up. "Anna! I was kidding, just kidding. I was . . . flirting. Badly, apparently."

It wasn't the joke or the flirting, it was last night's dream that made me turn my back. *Get a grip, Anna,* I told myself. *You can't blame someone for what he did in your dream.*

Zack picked up the sketchpad and pencil that had fallen off his lap. "Stay."

"Are you talking to me or Clyde?"

He laughed. "Clyde. And you. Would you like a soda? Or

some iced tea?" he offered. "Water with a slice of lime?" That's what he was drinking.

"No thanks. You look busy." One of the patio tables was covered with photos.

"Just sketching. Stick around. Clyde will be disappointed if you don't. How's Iris?" he asked.

"The same. How's Erika?" I replied, testing to see if the name in my dream was correct.

"Okay. How was work today?"

"It was interesting. I like Marcy."

"I'm glad. Do you like to stand when you talk to neighbors?"

I looked behind me, backed up to a chair, and sat. Zack laughed.

"Whatever I do seems to amuse you," I said.

"It's just that sometimes you're kind of fierce, and other times you're . . . very shy. I think that you are *actually* very shy."

"Maybe." I turned toward the water, but when I looked at it, all I saw was the color of Zack's eyes. "Can I take Clyde down to the creek?"

"Sure," he said. "Take him for a boat ride if you want."

"I can take the boat out, just Clyde and me?"

"That's what you'd prefer, isn't it?"

"Yes."

"You'll have to lift him in. Otherwise, he'll try to jump down to the boat and capsize it. Like someone else we know," Zack added slyly. "Put on a life jacket," he called as I headed toward the boat. "And avoid ducks."

Clyde stood patiently on the dock as I eased into the boat. He allowed me to lift him down, then settled in the center of the boat while I cast off.

I practiced rowing and felt good about my progress. I was finally getting the hang of it. After a while I slid down to the bottom of the boat next to Clyde, resting my back against the seat, drifting along, gazing at the streaky rose and violet sky. Clyde relaxed against my side, his tail lightly thumping against my thigh.

Suddenly, I felt him tense. I felt an upward surge of muscle, and short, strong legs pushing against me. The sound he made was one I'd never heard before, but I knew immediately it could summon people in red jackets on horseback. I grabbed him. The next moment the boat tipped, and Clyde and I and some very excited ducks were splashing around in the creek.

"Clyde, no! No, Clyde! Shoo, shoo!" I said to the ducks.

They flew up from the water, quacking their opinion of the dog and me. Clyde answered, baying for them to come back and play. Finally, he gave up and doggy-paddled toward shore.

I watched him all the way into the beach, then I swam

toward the boat. I knew Zack had heard Clyde's baying, but I kept my eyes on the rowboat, hoping that Zack would stay focused on his artwork.

Reaching the rowboat, I discovered that the little maneuver I had seen yesterday—Zack pulling himself up and over the side of the boat—required more arm strength than I had. After three tries, I considered swimming and towing the boat to the dock. But I wanted to get in the way a real boater would. I gave it one more try, propelling myself from the water, kicking till I got my body halfway over the bow, and flopping into the boat like an oversize flounder.

Hoping that Zack had not been watching, I moved onto the seat, pushed wet hair out of my eyes, and considered rowing around for a while as if nothing had happened. But I was exhausted and eager to get my feet on dry land. I rowed to the dock, where Zack was waiting with Clyde, the dog cheerfully wagging his little beagle tail.

Zack smiled but perhaps knew better than to crack a joke or act concerned. I silently looped the boat rope around the piling.

"Want a hand up?" he asked.

"Okay."

He reached down.

"Thank you." I stood on the dock, staring down at the boat. "There's water in it."

"Not much," he said in an easygoing way. "I'll clean up later."

"Thanks."

"Did you want to keep this?" he asked, and I felt his touch on my shoulder. I was wearing a slimy river weed.

"No, it doesn't look as good on land."

He smiled down at me, then tossed it into the water.

"When you said 'Avoid ducks,' I thought you meant don't *hit* the ducks—you know, like 'Avoid pedestrians.'"

He exploded with pent-up laughter. "Sorry. I understand. I should have been more specific," he said. "Come on, we keep towels just inside the terrace door." I walked beside him up the hill, accompanied by Clyde, who kept trying to lick the water off my legs.

The towel Zack handed me was big and soft. I wrapped myself in it and sat down in the same chair as before. "It's better if I stay over here and not drip on your stuff," I explained.

"Very thoughtful of you. Unnecessary, but thoughtful."

"So, what are you working on?"

"Just some sketches."

"Of what?" I asked.

He carried his chair over to mine with the sketchpad on its seat. As he opened it, I wondered if I was going to have to say those nice things artists like to hear. But as it turned out, I didn't have to be insincere; he was good, really good. Old oyster trawlers, crab pots, nets, men in heavy work gloves, piles of discarded shells, the carcass of a horseshoe crab. "Wow!"

The last three pages were efforts to draw a skipjack under sail, a workup of various angles. "Is this from the photographs over there?"

"Yeah, I have about a million of them. I just can't get it right. It looks like the boat is pasted to the sky. I can't get its movement."

I walked over to the table to look at the photographs, then came back to the sketchpad. "The colors and shading won't give the movement?"

"They'll help, but the lines are wrong. I'll get it, eventually. I love skipjacks. I love things that are both beautiful and useful."

I glanced up at him. "I love things that are beautiful when you don't expect them to be."

"Like what?" he asked softly.

"Oil rainbows on the road. Rain on a car windshield at night."

"Broken glass in sunlight?" he suggested.

"Yeah!" I met his eyes, then quickly looked down at the paper, pretending I was seeing his sketches rather than his eyes. "What, uh, medium do you work in?"

"Watercolor is my favorite, but it's the hardest. Do you paint?"

"Just walls and woodwork."

He laughed. "That's beautiful and useful."

I was starting to like his laugh.

"Are you dating anybody?" His blunt question caught me off guard.

"Uh . . . no." I felt vulnerable. I reminded myself of last night's dream. Dream or not, Erika was real. "No, I'm looking for a jock."

"A jock! Why do girls always chase sweaty guys?"

"I don't know why the others do, but I have a lousy track record with artistic types."

"Oh."

"A writer, a musician, and a visual artist. That was my senior year."

"Really. Did you date the artist for long?"

"Till ten o'clock the night before my senior prom."

"Ouch."

"When artists need an audience, they find me. And then later on . . ."

Zack quickly closed the sketchpad. "You don't think jocks are looking for an audience?"

"The difference is, they're up front about it. They don't pretend to be falling in love with the soul of a girl."

He gazed at me steadily, as if he could see into my soul.

"Jocks don't say and do all those romantic things—probably because they don't know how—and then drop you for some hot girl who carries her soul in a purse."

"I see."

I stood up. "I should check on Aunt Iris. Thanks for the towel. I'll bring it back clean."

"Just leave it here," Zack replied. "I'll throw it in the wash."

But my clothes were wet and clinging to me. "No, it's not a problem," I said, and headed home, holding on to my security towel. If only it were as easy to keep my heart safely wrapped up.

Eleven

TIRED FROM MY first day of work and the swim in the creek, I fell asleep quickly Tuesday night. When I opened my eyes again, I lay in darkness. I waited for the low, vibrating sound, my fingers gripping the edge of the mattress. A bead of sweat trickled down my face. I turned my head to dry my cheek on the pillow, then sat up slowly. I could move, which meant the strange experience wasn't happening. My alarm clock read 4:08. What had awakened me? I climbed out of bed and turned off the fan to listen. The house was silent, as if waiting to exhale.

Then I heard Aunt Iris's voice. I tiptoed through Uncle Will's room to the hall. The first floor was dark, but Aunt Iris was there, in the living room, I thought. She was arguing with someone. I couldn't hear the other person's response, just furious rushes of words from my aunt with long pauses in between.

"I'm tired of your opinions," I heard Aunt Iris say. "I'm sick of you telling me what to do."

There was a moment of quiet, enough time for someone to respond, then she went on: "You don't understand, William. You couldn't possibly, you're a man."

William? Was she reliving an old argument with Uncle Will or having a new one with a wooden post? I crept down the steps.

"We have enough room, enough money," she insisted. "I've made up my mind. We're keeping the child."

I paused mid-step: This was an argument about me.

"It's not interfering!" Iris said, her voice getting shrill. "It's loving. Don't you understand? Someone had to say something to her. It may as well have been me."

There was another silence, a long one.

"How dare you blame me for that! How dare you, William!"

I couldn't tell if this was one argument or several mixed together. I didn't know if "her" was myself or my mother. Reaching the bottom of the stairs, I flicked the light switch. Aunt Iris was in the living room, standing five feet from the grandfather clock, staring at its luminous face, her hands clenched.

I didn't know what she heard or saw, but she suddenly buried her face in her hands and began to cry. "I did what I thought was best." Her crying became louder. "Stop it, *stop it*. I don't care what you think!" She began to sob.

"Aunt Iris," I said, moving quickly to her side. "Aunt Iris, it's me, Anna." I pulled on her hands, trying to get them away from her face so she would see it was just us there, but her arms were surprisingly strong. She kept her face hidden and continued to cry.

"Everything's okay. It's just a—a dream," I said. "You're having a dream. Aunt Iris, can you hear me? Look at me." I pulled on her fingers.

Quick as a cat, she struck, making long scratches down my arm. I stepped back, surprised, rubbing my raw skin.

"Aunt Iris, it's just a *stupid clock*!"

The crying lessened. Spreading her fingers, she looked through them like a child, peering anxiously at the tall clock's face.

I walked up to it. "See, it's ticking and has a pendulum, and hands that show—" I broke off, aware of a strange cold that emanated from the area in front of the clock. The skin on the back of my neck rose in goose bumps.

Crossing my arms over my chest, I walked toward a window, then returned to the clock and walked toward the open hall door, trying to find a source for a draft. The air was stale, motionless, warm—except in front of the clock. I shivered.

"Stop blaming me, William," Iris said bitterly. "I had no choice. Do you hear me?"

I stared at the clock: painted numbers, hands like delicate

arrows, a gold moon setting in its crescent-shaped window. What was she seeing that I couldn't?

Her voice began to rise in pitch. "Listen to me!" Her body trembled with anger. "Why don't you listen to me?" she screamed, and charged the clock, slamming against it, making it rock.

I tried to drag her back from the heavy piece, afraid she would pull it down on herself. I couldn't loosen her grip. The strength in her arms and hands seemed unnatural.

Uncle Will, I prayed silently, *please stop. Please go. Please leave her in peace.*

A second later Aunt Iris ceased struggling. Her shoulders hunched and her hands hung limply at her sides. I eased her into a nearby chair. She sat silently, head bowed, knees together, one bare foot crossed on top of the other.

I stood next to her, shaking—after my spontaneous prayer I had felt the cold drain from the air. I paced back and forth in front of the clock. The air was warm now; only my skin felt cold and clammy.

"He's left," Aunt Iris said.

"I—I couldn't see him."

"I could. He's gone."

"You fought a lot with Uncle Will, didn't you?"

"He was my older brother. Papa died when I was eighteen.

William came back from the war and started acting as if he were my father too."

"And my grandmother, your sister, she wasn't around?"

"JoEllen was ten years older than William," Aunt Iris explained. "She hated the Shore and moved out of the house at seventeen, moved to Philadelphia and married twice—came back here only once. She brought your mother when Joanna was a young teenager. Perhaps JoEllen foresaw that she would get cancer and her daughter would need us one day." Closing her eyes, Iris rested her head against the high back of the chair. Her big hands hung heavily off its carved arms. She breathed slowly, deeply. She was exhausted.

"Maybe we should get a little more sleep," I said. "Come on, Aunt Iris, I'll help you upstairs."

Although she wouldn't let me take her arm, she walked with me. Outside her bedroom door, she stopped, looking lost.

"This is your room. Would you like to go in?"

Her mouth worked, but she said nothing.

"Or maybe you would like to talk for a few minutes," I suggested. "Are there some things you want to talk about?"

"I can't."

"Maybe tomorrow."

Her hands became agitated, her fingers plucking at her tattered nightgown. "I can't tell you. I can't tell you!"

"You can't tell me . . . about something from the past?"

"Past, future, it's all one."

"Sometimes it helps to talk."

She shook her head. "There are secrets I can never tell."

"Well, maybe not the secret part, but it might help to—"

"Never, never, never!"

"Okay." I'd had enough. If she needed to talk, there was always tomorrow. "Try to get some sleep. G'night." I headed down the hall to the entrance of Uncle Will's room, aware that she was watching me. When I reached the door, I turned back and saw a suspicious look on her face.

"Why are you going in William's room?"

"Because that is how I get to the other room, where my bed is, where you left the fan," I added, hoping it would jog her memory.

She narrowed her eyes. "You're searching for something."

"I'm going to bed, and I think you should too."

"I can't."

I sighed and retraced my steps. Squeezing past her, I entered her bedroom and turned on a small lamp. She followed me into the room as far as her bureau, stopping suddenly, looking fearfully into the mirror that hung above it.

Her bed hadn't been slept in. I pulled down the covers and plumped the pillows, trying to make it look inviting. She watched, facing me, then turned away to watch me in the mirror. She looked at me directly again and turned a second time to the mirror image, as if she thought she were seeing two different images and couldn't decide which one was real. She was giving me the creeps.

"Your bed is ready," I told her.

"You're on his side."

"What?"

"It's the two of you against me," she insisted, looking at me through the mirror.

"Who?" I asked, although I guessed that she meant Uncle Will and me.

"Don't play dumb! You and William are trying to get rid of me. You want to push me out of my home. You want this place for yourselves."

I walked across the room to her. "Aunt Iris, I have a home in Baltimore, and I'll be going away to college in August. I'm not going to push you out of your home."

"You think I'm crazy," she said.

When I didn't respond, she whirled around to face me directly. The anger in her eyes made me take a step back.

"You want to send me away."

"That's not why I'm here," I replied. "I came for a visit."

She turned back to my reflection in the mirror. "I don't like what I see." The way she peered into the glass made the mirror seem as deep as Oyster Creek. "I don't like it at all." Her fingers curled around a hairbrush with a silver handle. She lifted it slowly, her eyes locking on mine in the mirror. Inch by inch, she pulled back her arm, as if fearing too quick a movement would give her away. The ornate back of the brush glimmered in the lamplight. She slammed it against the glass. The mirror shattered, fragments of our reflections dropping onto her bureau.

For a moment Aunt Iris seemed as stunned as I by what she had done. I grabbed the brush from her, then scooped up the matching hand mirror and retreated from her room. Knowing she still had lamps and other potential weapons, I pulled the door closed behind me, pausing for a moment in the hall, listening for activity inside her room. Hearing none, I continued on to mine. I debated whether to shove a piece of furniture against my door. I assumed I could outrun her, but if I fell asleep and she came in . . .

I could no longer deny it: If the right object were in her hand, Aunt Iris was capable of killing someone. It frightened me because I didn't know what she saw, what she *thought* she saw when she looked at me, or the mirror, or the grandfather clock. I could only guess at what would set her off.

I considered calling the sheriff, but I knew that neither he nor anyone else had the power to whisk her away to a psychiatric hospital, not if she wasn't willing to go. She'd have to do something clearly life-threatening, and even then, they'd probably just stick her in the hospital for a day or two and medicate her. Afterward, I'd be bringing her back here—spitting mad.

Mom would know how to handle this kind of thing, and she would be back in ten days. I just needed to hang on till then.

I didn't bother to barricade the attic—there wasn't much chance of me falling back asleep. Outside, the sky was growing lighter. At twenty minutes after five I crept to Iris's room and quietly opened the door. She was sleeping soundly.

I returned to my own room and dozed for the next two hours, then was awakened suddenly by the loud creak of my door.

"Just me," Aunt Iris called cheerfully.

I sat up quickly, hitting my head on the ceiling.

"The sun is up. It's a lovely day."

"Great," I muttered, swinging my feet down to the floor, resting my arms on my knees, more tired now than when I had gone to bed. I watched her carry the broken mirror past my corner of the attic room, placing it with the cemetery of smashed television sets.

This had happened before; it would happen again.

Twelve

ALWAYS CHRISTMAS WAS a world apart from Aunt Iris's house, and as soon as I entered the shop, I felt better. Marcy and I got along well, maybe because I liked to work hard. About three o'clock that afternoon, when the temperature and humidity had soared high enough to keep vacationers inside whatever air-cooled place they'd found, the sleigh bells on the door stopped jingling. Marcy perched on a stool behind a counter, paging through wholesale catalogs, circling items. I picked up a spray bottle and attacked smudgy surfaces.

"Audrey mentioned meeting you two nights ago," Marcy said. "I'd be willing to bet you had an interesting conversation."

I glanced across the room at her and detected a smile. "Yes. When Uncle Will invited me, he didn't tell me I'd be living in a house of evil."

She laughed. "That's Audrey for you. My friends find her very strange and wonder why I keep her on."

"Why do you?"

"Loyalty. She worked for my parents and was very good to me when I was growing up." Marcy turned a page, then looked up. "You and I have something in common. I was adopted. Most people would consider it lucky to be me, adopted by a wealthy family like the Fairfaxes. It would have been, except that my mother later gave birth to a son, one who happened to look like the portraits of every firstborn male Fairfax since the seventeenth century. They nearly worshipped at the crib."

"That doesn't sound good, for him or you."

"It wasn't for me. Unfortunately, getting into trouble was the one way I could get my parents' attention. Audrey looked past the stupid things I did. While the other servants enjoyed reporting those things to my parents and making our relationship worse, Audrey always tried to make it better. I guess she figured it was her job to save me and took me on as her mission in life." Marcy smiled wryly. "I certainly kept her busy."

"I hope she doesn't make *me* her next mission. Marcy, are there other people in Wisteria who think Aunt Iris is in league with the devil?"

She thought about the question. "A few, probably, because of her reputation as a psychic. People fear anyone who differs from what is considered normal, and in a small town the idea of normal can be as narrow as the streets."

"Did anyone fear my mother?"

"Why would they?"

"She was psychic."

"I knew she lived with Iris and William, but I was away at college when she moved in. She died in a robbery, didn't she? How old were you?"

"Barely three. I don't really remember her. When Uncle Will asked me to come, he said he wanted to tell me about my family. He said there were some things that he needed to explain."

Marcy nodded and turned a page, her eyes on the catalog. The fact that she didn't study me with the overly concerned expression of a school guidance counselor encouraged me. "I need to ask you a question."

She waited a moment, her pen holding her place on the page. "No point in backing out now."

"Aunt Iris can get angry, crazy angry. You heard what the elf man said yesterday. Do you think she could have killed Uncle Will?"

"No." Marcy circled an item in the catalog, then looked up. "I don't believe Iris is capable of really harming someone. She's just not that kind of person, Anna. I would worry about her health, but not that she's a murderer."

She flipped the page of the catalog. "Oh, my." She brought

over the book to show me the picture she had been looking at. "How do you like these?"

"Leprechaun angels?"

"Handsome, aren't they? I could probably sell a bushel of them and turn a nice profit, but I do have some pride."

"I didn't know leprechauns were that big an item."

"It's angels. People collect them. I could sell an angelic choir wearing fatigues and riding in Humvees."

"I like the ones by Cindy Reed."

"Me too, but I'm afraid that's the last of them. Cindy took her newest set of Christmas figures to Jeanette's Crafts, showed them to Jeanette before she showed them to me."

I walked over to the shelf of wooden angels. I was hoping to buy one for Mom's Christmas gift.

Marcy returned to her perch. "Loyalty is very important in retail. Sometimes it is the only thing one can rely on. Unfortunately, Cindy doesn't know what I know. Jeanette's lease is up next year and she's planning to retire. Cindy will be out of luck—I'm not buying from her again."

Having no experience in business, I wasn't going to argue, but it seemed kind of senseless to me to stop carrying a product that customers bought, just because someone else got first choice.

Marcy laughed. "Your face is an open book. I admit, I have

a healthy streak of pride in me, and I am the kind of person who likes to know whom I can rely on. I built this business out of nothing. My parents, with all their money, didn't loan me a nickel—they thought I couldn't pull it off."

"That must have been hard."

"Yes, but most things that are satisfying *are* hard. Don't let others tell you that you can't have what you want, Anna. Go after it."

"Most of the time I do."

As I turned away from the shelf of angels, I glanced out the window. Zack was coming down the street, carrying cardboard mailing tubes and wearing the preppy office clothes I had seen him in before. When he started up the steps to Marcy's shop, I quickly looked for another piece of glass to polish.

The sleigh bells jingled.

"Hi, Marcy. Hi, Anna."

"Well, this is a nice surprise," Marcy said to Zack. "Is everything all right with your father?"

"Yes, I'm delivering some blueprints for him, and I thought I'd stop by."

"You never stopped by before," she observed.

"I never realized what great air-conditioning you had," he answered smoothly. "I may have to come more often."

"Uh-huh."

He flashed his stepmother a grin, then walked over to me. "Actually, I came because I have a last-minute invitation. My friend Erika Gill is having a big party tomorrow night, one of those all-out birthday bashes that girls like. Want to go?"

For a moment all I could do was stare at him. *This is just a coincidence,* I told myself. But in my gut I didn't believe it. What I had dreamed two nights ago was somehow becoming real, just like the fire. He was carrying out the drama queen's request to date me.

"No. Sorry."

"Since it's a catered thing, at a restaurant, I'll pick you up at—what did you say?"

"I'm sorry. I can't do it."

Behind his back, Marcy watched, her eyes bright.

"You're busy?"

"I just can't do it," I said.

"Maybe she has a boyfriend, Zack," Marcy suggested.

"She doesn't," he replied quickly, then bit his lip. "I mean, it's just that we talked about that last night."

Was that why he had asked the question? Was last night also part of carrying out Erika's plan?

"I thought you might like meeting new people," he said.

"Will there be any cute jocks?"

He looked irritated. "Yeah, sure, if that's what you want."

What I wanted was to stop falling for guys who acted interested in me, when really . . .

"Maybe another time," I said, and turned back to a display of glass figures.

When he left, Marcy shook her head in amazement. "Now I have seen everything. Zack never gets turned down. He needs a secretary to keep track of all the girls."

"Then he'll get over it."

"Why did you say no?" Marcy asked. "It's none of my business, but I can't help but be curious. I hope it wasn't because I was here."

"It wasn't." I picked up a skinny Santa and polished his boot.

"Are you playing hard to get?"

"No."

Marcy studied me, head tilted. "Well, I'm glad someone has finally said no to him. Being motherless and an only child, Zack is used to getting one hundred percent of his father's attention, which I understand, but it isn't good for him. And he is so popular with kids his own age, he expects everyone to do whatever he wants. This time, someone didn't. You're a different kind of girl, Anna."

"I guess so."

Playing hard to get? A guy had to be interested in you before you could play hard to get.

When I arrived home that evening, Aunt Iris and her gold Chevrolet were gone. I found two large trays of cat food and a scattering of nuggets on the kitchen floor, indicating she had recently fed the herd and let them out again. I fixed dinner and carried it into Uncle Will's den. Two cats were sleeping on the porch, and I lured them inside with scraps from my plate, trusting them to tell me when Aunt Iris was coming home.

I sat at Uncle Will's big oak desk, eating a chef's salad and planning my search. The wall across from the fireplace was lined from floor to ceiling with shelves. Books, magazines, and newspapers were crammed between the shelves and piled on the floor next to an old leather chair, where Uncle Will must have read. The papers on the desk and things on the floor were neatly stacked, perhaps the result of a police search. But it didn't look as if the stuffed bookshelves had been touched.

I began with the desk, rifling quickly through old bank records, canceled checks, and outdated warrantees. When I opened the last drawer, I stopped. It was filled with photos, pictures of my birth mother and me: me with a tricycle, me with an inner tube, several photos of me with a fishing rod. I had my own copies of the photos that included my mother, but seeing them here, in the place where we had lived together, made the woman in the pictures more real. Even I was struck by the resemblance between us, especially since I was almost as old as she had been in the photos. If I wore my hair up as she did, we could have passed for twins.

Finding no important documents in the desk, I turned to the wall of shelves. In my study nook at home, I tended to stick things on the shelves closest to where I was sitting. Since Uncle Will's desk backed up to the wall, making some of the shelves within easy reaching distance, I decide to start three shelves from the bottom, then work progressively above and below that shelf, going from most accessible to least. Removing each book in turn, I flipped through it, hoping to find loose papers. If there was something in this room about my mother or family, something Uncle Will had wanted me to know, I was going to find it.

Most of Uncle Will's books were about Maryland, the two World Wars, and wildlife, some of the volumes quite old. He must have subscribed to every fishing and outdoorsman magazine in existence. The magazines and newspapers were stuffed between the tops of the books and the next shelf up. I removed one newspaper, skimmed it, and finally found an article on a fishing charter service out of Wisteria, which may have been the reason Uncle Will had saved it. Realizing it would take forever to go through all the newspapers looking for the reason they had been kept, I began to stack them on the floor with the plan to go through them when I had completed my search of the den.

As I removed book after book, I stopped reading the titles. Then I noticed one with pictures different from battlefields and shorebirds: mug shots. I thumbed back to the title page: *Psychosis and the Criminal Mind*. Well, that was interesting! I glanced at the binding of the next book: *Famous Psychotics*. I pulled it out, turned to its table of contents, and scanned the chapter headings: Criminals, Kings, Scientists, Musicians, Writers, Actors, Mediums. There was a penciled check next to the first and final chapters. Aunt Iris probably considered herself a medium, a channel for thought and feelings from "the other side." I hoped she wasn't a criminal. Continuing down the row of books, I found *A History of Psychosis and Healing*. I guess it wasn't surprising that Uncle Will had an interest in mental illness. There were three more thick books on it, then the topic changed. *You and the Paranormal,* I read. He had about a dozen books on that subject.

I completed two shelves, petted the sleeping cats, telling them to keep up the good work, then moved on to a third. Halfway through it, I pulled out a wad of newspaper that was lighter in color than the others. Figuring it was more recent, I checked the date: May 22, one day before Uncle Will had written his letter inviting me to Wisteria.

I reviewed it carefully but found nothing that appeared related to him or Aunt Iris. Setting it aside, I pulled out the books beneath where it had been crammed. Another wad of newspaper came out with them, this one toast-colored—old. At first I thought that the wad was nothing more than neatly folded paper, then I realized something was wrapped inside it. I knew that the tape on the wrapping had been broken recently, because it had left behind white stripes. I carefully removed the layers of dry paper and found an old notebook with soft covers.

Fingers trembling, guessing that this was something important, I opened the book. My mother's name was inscribed on the inside cover. I touched the ink, then traced her handwriting, as if I could read the person who wrote it in the slashes and curves of her letters. The phone number listed beneath her name belonged to Uncle Will and Aunt Iris—she had used this book when I was part of her life.

The first sheet was headed "Appointments," the information beneath it written in neat columns: month, day, time of day, followed by initials. Many of the listings bore the designation "Paid." It must have been my mother's client book. I wondered why she had used initials; perhaps some people didn't want it known that they were seeing a psychic adviser.

The entries ran for at least ten pages, with blank sheets following. As I flipped through them, a piece of unlined paper slipped out. I unfolded it and read what appeared to be a poem:

> The seed cracks open, the green sprout
> of a plant emerges—
> a green snake.
> The snake slides past a rabbit,
> glides past a cat.
> Winding itself around flowers—
> a garden shaped like a heart—
> the snake turns to me.
> It wears a mask.
> Flowers wilt.

I read it three times, trying to understand what my mother was saying, finding it even more cryptic than the poems written by my old boyfriend. Slipping the paper back into the book, I flipped to the back cover. My mother had written down dates on which term papers were due and several names and phone numbers. One was labeled "Chase College," where she was taking courses. Another said "Pharmacy." The third belonged to someone named Elliot Gill. *Gill*—Erika's last name. Were they related? It was, after all, a small town.

Although the cats gave no sign of Aunt Iris's imminent

arrival, I rewrapped the notebook and placed it back where I had found it, worried that if I left it out, Aunt Iris might sweep it up in one of her angry displays. It occurred to me that Uncle Will may have shared that concern. Perhaps he was interrupted while examining the notebook and hastily slipped it behind the other books, hiding it with whatever newspaper was handy, the newspaper from that day. I wondered if there was something he had read in the notebook that caused him to write to me the next day and ask me to come.

I sat back in his chair, thinking I had made a big mistake. Because my feelings were hurt by Zack, I had passed up an opportunity to get to know the girl who appeared to be responsible for the fire. I was like Marcy with her response to Cindy Reed and her beautiful angels, forgetting my ultimate goal. And it wasn't just contact with Erika that I would be missing out on. Kids talked at parties, boasting and gossiping; chances were good that I could learn something from some of her friends who had been at the fire. I owed it to Uncle Will to find out how he had died. And I had come here to learn whatever he needed to tell me about my mother and her family. If Elliot Gill was important enough to have his number listed in my mother's book, he might know something. The truth was, I had more reasons to go with Zack to the party than he had to go with me. "Two can play this game," I said aloud, and headed for Zack's house.

Thirteen

AUDREY ANSWERED THE door. Either I had a grim look on my face or she had a genuine obsession with the "House of Evil."

"I knew something terrible would happen," she said. "Come in, child. As soon as I finish with the family's dinner, we can talk."

"Nothing has happened," I told her. "I just want to speak to Zack."

"Who is it, Audrey?" a man called, and a moment later emerged through a door beneath a sweeping stairway. "Hello."

He had the same body structure and the same basic coloring as Zack, though his hair was a shade lighter and his blue eyes lacked the haunting depth of Zack's. Those differences and a slightly rounder face made him pleasant-looking rather than handsome. "I'm Dave Fleming, Zack's dad. You must be Anna."

"Yes, how did you know?"

"By the"—he hesitated—"chestnut-colored hair."

Zack must have told him about that. "I'll come back. I don't want to interrupt your dinner."

"It's not an interruption, it's a visit. Come in, come in," he said, gesturing toward the door through which he had just come. "Have you had dinner? We'll set another place at the table. Audrey's a fabulous cook."

"Thanks, but I've already eaten. I just need to speak to Zack for a second."

Audrey exited through a small door. I was hoping Dave would call Zack, but instead, he led me through the door beneath the curved stairway. We emerged into a dusky, high-ceilinged dining room. Zack and Marcy sat at the far end of a polished table that looked long enough to bowl on. Both of them appeared surprised, the flickering candlelight exaggerating their expressions. Zack put down his fork and rose politely to his feet, which made me feel as if I were in a Jane Austen novel. His father strode ahead of me and carried a chair over to the table, setting it next to Zack's.

"Really, I've had dinner, sir."

"Dave," Zack's father corrected me, smiling. "Call me Dave."

"I'm just staying a minute."

"But you can't," Dave protested. "I'm the only one in the family who hasn't gotten the opportunity to know you. Marcy sings your praises. Zack tells me . . . a few things."

"Dad," Zack said with a note of warning.

"According to Audrey, even Clyde has conversed with you—in dog language."

Marcy rolled her eyes.

"And a goat, too, apparently." From a drawer in a massive sideboard, Dave drew out a place mat and silverware. "If you've had dinner, I'm sure you would like dessert."

"Thanks but—"

"Strawberries and whipped cream, guaranteed to contribute to heart disease and—"

"Dearest," Marcy interrupted, "Anna knows what she wants and doesn't want."

"Oh. Well, then, I suppose that is why you two get along so well," he said, gazing lovingly at his wife. He turned back to me. "Please sit down. Perhaps you would like something chocolate instead. I'm sure we have—"

"Dad," Zack said, "she's not hungry. She doesn't want to sit down. Let her talk."

"Of course." Dave sat down at the same time as Zack and waited.

"I've changed my mind. I'd like to go to the party tomorrow."

In the candlelight Marcy's eyes glinted. She probably thought I had joined the army of girls chasing Zack. But Zack didn't; the expression on his face was guarded, thoughtful, as if he was deducing my motive.

"I mean, if you haven't asked someone else," I added.

"I haven't."

"Well, then, that's settled," Dave said, jumping into the awkward moment. "It's always good to meet new people— Zack to meet you, you to meet others, that kind of thing."

Zack took a sip of water from his cut-glass goblet, barely hiding his smirk. "I'll pick you up at seven forty-five," he said. "Since it's catered, we're supposed to arrive on time."

"I'll be ready." I took a step back. "Nice meeting you . . . Dave. I really have to go. Don't anyone get up. I know where the door is." I pivoted and almost took out Audrey, who had entered through a side door. "Sorry." I gave her a little wave, then exited.

When I returned to the house, Aunt Iris and her gold car were still absent. I was uncomfortable with her there, and yet just as uncomfortable with her gone. I couldn't say whether it was Iris's safety I feared for or the safety of those she might become angry with, including me. She was strong. And I had seen firsthand how easy it was for her to disconnect with reality. It wasn't as simple as believing, the way Marcy did, that Iris wasn't the *kind* of person who could harm someone; psychotics turned into other kinds of people.

The Back Door of Midnight

I needed to do some research, and Uncle Will's collection of books would provide a good start. I pulled from his shelves several of the books I had noticed earlier and carried them upstairs, trailed by one of the two cats I had hired as lookouts. As soon as I set down the books, the little silver tabby leaped onto my bed. I let her stay, liking the company, hoping she didn't have fleas.

I began with the book on famous psychotic criminals, paging through it, studying the pictures. Some of the men and women looked nearly possessed, but others appeared as normal and pleasant as Dave Fleming—well, that was reassuring! I read a few case histories and, after a particularly gruesome account, set the text aside. Opening a book on the paranormal, I surveyed its table of contents: Telepathy, Clairvoyance, Precognition, Psychokinesis, Out-of-Body Experiences, Mediumship—I backed up. *Out-of-Body Experiences*— meaning experiences when you didn't seem to have a body? Experiences when your hands were as transparent as jellyfish? I quickly flipped to the chapter.

I turned on the lamp and for the next hour read that chapter and a similar one in another book, reading the material twice, amazed by the accuracy with which the writers were able to describe my own weird experiences. Having a name for the occurrence, which was often referred to by the acronym O.B.E., made it seem less frightening.

According to the authors, vibrations and electrical sensations were commonly reported in the early stages of an O.B.E., as was the temporary paralysis I had experienced. Some people heard electrical sounds, others, loud rushing noises, which were attributed to the spirit leaving the body through its "chakras." There was one notable difference between the experience that most people reported and my own: I hadn't had the shock of looking down at my own body sleeping. Nor had I enjoyed flying and choosing where I would go, an experience that some people described to researchers. It was as if the moment I let go, I was launched on a mission—as if I had been summoned by someone and was under that person's guidance. Uncle Will? There were stories about O.B.E.s in which the "astral traveler" saw relatives who had died.

Parapsychologists believed that, when out of body, people perceived with their minds, not their physical senses. However, they often interpreted their perceptions the only way they knew how, as if they had five physical senses. Out of body, without physical limitations, their minds "saw" 360 degrees around them, but since humans aren't used to seeing that, the images seemed to overlap and became confusing when the perceiver tried to interpret them. Also, they saw things that physical eyes couldn't see—other forms of energy—which produced distortions in the mindscape.

A week ago, reading this stuff, I would have laughed. None of it was scientifically proven. But when you're having really weird experiences and two writers describe them in detail, you're ready to believe whatever explanation they offer.

Both writers claimed that astral travelers could improve their perceptions by saying things like "I want to see more clearly now." I remembered how I had made my vision clearer during my last two experiences: I complained to Aunt Iris, saying that I needed to see. I had assumed that she had cleared my vision, but perhaps the power was within me. That was the most interesting part of what I read in the books: the ability of the person having the O.B.E. to control the experience. Some people learned to induce out-of-body experiences and used them for "astral exploration." Could I control my experiences enough to learn the details of Uncle Will's death?

One of the books explained how to put yourself in a super-relaxed stage with the goal of inducing an O.B.E. I tried it. I took deep breaths and imagined myself floating; I stared at a lamp; I lit a candle; I focused on the soothing purr of my tabby friend and hummed along. I told my feet, knees, hips, and arms that they were very, very heavy, but nothing worked. An hour later I blew out the candle and lay back in the darkness, frustrated. In my everyday life I knew how to go after what I wanted, but I was no good at letting go and having things come to me.

That's when I heard it—not a low, throbbing sound, but a squeak—metal rubbing against wood. The cat raised her head. The noise had come from outside. I heard it twice, as if something had opened and closed. The cat leaped lightly off the bed and padded past the bureaus toward the far end of the attic room. I followed her to the last window, the one above Uncle Will's den. She sprang into the casement and peered down. I knelt next to her, pressing my face against the screen.

At first I thought Aunt Iris had come home and was burying more ashes, for the figure below was bent over the spot marked by the knife. Then that person stepped back to gaze up at the house. I ducked, but I had already glimpsed the halo of white hair. Audrey.

Using the kitty as camouflage, I snatched a second look and saw that Audrey was holding a bag from which she took objects not much bigger than her fists. She arranged them on the ground, working quickly, then headed back through the gate in the hedge, opening and shutting it with a double squeak.

I moved like the cat, stealing down the back steps to Uncle Will's den, and exited through the door on the creek side. After the darkness inside the house, the moonlit night seemed bright. In the area marked by the knife, rows of painted rocks gleamed. The cat circled the area, then sniffed the individual rocks. They were smooth and round, like stones that had been purchased from a store rather than dug out of a garden. Each one bore a black cross or *X* on it, hand-painted, judging by the uneven strokes.

Whether the symbol was religious or simply an *X*, I could guess what it meant. In school we had read about the burial practices of various cultures, some of which used rocks to "keep" the dead person in his or her place. Audrey had made sure that William couldn't rise out of his ashes to haunt her. Did she fear him that much? It seemed crazy to fear someone whom I remembered as a little stern but very caring. I stared at the butcher knife that marked the grave, wondering if I had known Uncle Will as well as I thought.

I pulled out the knife, then grabbed the shovel that Iris had left leaning against the house. I'd assumed she had buried the jar of ashes, and Audrey had assumed I knew what I was talking about. But what if there was something different under the dirt, like a heavy object that could bludgeon someone to death or an object that could kill when knocked over accidentally?

I dug in a fury, and the cat watched with interest at first. Twenty minutes later I leaned on the shovel, astounded at how deep Aunt Iris had dug. The sandy earth, having been lifted out recently, was loose, but it was probably packed hard for her. I was nearly three feet down and still hadn't found anything. Was this just a hoax? The cat had departed, but I was so intent on getting to the bottom of the hole, I forgot what that meant. I kept digging. I had just uncovered the Skippy peanut butter lid when I heard Aunt Iris's car.

I gazed down at the top of the jar, trying to decide what to do. I could dash up to the attic room, using the back steps from Uncle Will's den. If questioned, I could say I saw Audrey digging here. But lying would only complicate things. I stood still and waited to see lights come on in the house. None did. I drummed my fingers against the handle of the shovel, my eyes scanning the windows. Aunt Iris's pale face appeared at the screen door of Uncle Will's den.

"Hi," I said. "I was wondering when you would get home."

"I think you were hoping I would not."

I glanced down at the hole. "Well, maybe not until I finished here."

She emerged onto the top step. "The dead should rest in peace."

"Can they, if they've been murdered?"

Her mouth twitched and she gazed off into the distance, as if she were reading the answer there. "Perhaps not."

I picked up the shovel, deciding to complete my task. She watched quietly as I unearthed the jar of ashes. Something else was in the hole, something that gleamed in the moonlight. I reached down.

So, Aunt Iris had found Erika's cell phone.

"Audrey's been here," Iris observed.

"Yes." I gestured toward the stones with one hand and pocketed the phone with the other. "She brought those over and placed them on top of the hole. I came out to see what she was doing."

"She was sticking her nose in my business, that's what she was doing!"

"Is she afraid of Uncle Will—I mean, the dead Uncle Will?"

I saw the glint in Iris's eye, the tiny smile of satisfaction. "Could be."

I carried the jar over to her. "Aunt Iris, how do you know the ashes in here are his? How do you know they're not just pieces of the car, burned-up seats and carpeting?"

"I can sense it."

"But how?"

"How do you know the ashes are gray?" she asked back.

"I can see them."

"If you worked a little harder, Joanna, you could see more," she said.

"I'm Anna, and I'm not psychic."

"You're an O'Neill and a girl. You have little choice."

"All right, I'm not going to argue. Can you sense who killed Uncle Will?"

Her eyes widened for a moment, then narrowed again, becoming a defiant stare.

"Can you?" I persisted.

"Do him the courtesy of putting him back."

"Can you sense *where* he was killed? Can you sense *when*?"

"I won't," she replied, pressing her lips together, then turned and headed into the house.

I pulled Erika's cell phone out of my pocket. I knew I should give it to the sheriff immediately, but I wanted to check it out. The battery was shot, and my charger wouldn't work with an iPhone. My iPod's would . . . except I'd lent it to Mom for vacation. So I'd spring for a charger—it was worth it.

I slipped the phone back into my pocket, then deposited "Uncle Will" in the hole, finding it a lot easier to pile dirt in than to dig it out. When finished, I placed the stones back on the plot the way Audrey had arranged them. If I returned the stones to her, confronting her with her strange actions, or got rid of them by throwing them in the river, she would probably have to devise some other way to make herself feel safe. People do crazy things when they believe they are threatened, and I wasn't going to encourage any more craziness than we already had around here.

Fourteen

THURSDAY NIGHT I wore the only glam sundress I had brought with me. At 7:45, I found Zack on the front porch talking with Aunt Iris. She was giggling, batting her eyelashes, and trying to pat her wild red hair into place.

When I stepped onto the porch, Zack turned to me. "Hey. You look good."

"Thanks. Where's your car?"

"At home. I thought we'd leave from my house rather than . . . rather than block in Iris."

Rather than lose your muffler, I thought.

"Rather than lose your muffler," Aunt Iris said with a flirty laugh.

Zack blinked. "That, too," he admitted, then turned and smiled into my eyes. "I'm glad you decided to go tonight."

I drew back. *Even though it was Erika, not you, who wanted me to come.*

"Even though it was—"

"Aunt Iris," I interrupted her.

She tapped me on the hand. "I wouldn't let that kind of thing bother you."

Zack glanced from her to me, trying to understand what had just passed between us, then his gaze dropped to my feet and he started smiling again. "I *thought* you looked taller. I'll get the car. I didn't know you'd be wearing fancy girl shoes."

What did you think I'd wear, Uncle Will's hip boots?

"William's hip boots are in his boat," Aunt Iris said to me with a sad shake of her head. "The police have them now."

Zack looked bewildered.

I probably looked irritated by his response to my shoes, because he added suddenly, "What I meant to say is that you look really nice tonight, really nice in those shoes. Not that it's unusual. I mean, you always look nice. But tonight you look . . . fancy and nice and—"

"You told me the party was at a restaurant," I said, feeling my cheeks get pink. "I thought people would dress up. You did."

To my surprise, *his* cheeks grew pink.

"Can we just go?" I asked, removing my tall heels to carry them.

"Sure. Yeah. Let's go."

"Bye, Aunt Iris."

"Have a wonderful time, Joanna."

When we were out of earshot, he asked, "Is your full name Joanna?"

"No. Sometimes Aunt Iris thinks I'm my birth mother."

We walked in silence to the edge of the O'Neill property. As we passed through the gate, Zack leaned toward me. "My dad's on the terrace. If we stick close to the trees, we won't have to stop and talk to him."

"But I want dessert," I whispered back.

Zack grinned.

"And, anyway, I think he's nice," I added.

"So do I," Zack replied, his smile softening.

We skirted the house. I wanted to keep on walking with him—not go to the party, just walk with him and make him smile again. I reminded myself this was not a date, but a mission, for both him and me.

"How long has your dad been married to Marcy?"

"Two years. He built this house for her."

"It's new?" I turned to study it, walking backward a few steps.

"Yeah. Dad's an architect. She wanted a new but colonial-looking mansion, and that's what she got."

"It's beautiful."

He shrugged. "I liked the old house where he and I lived the first year we came to Wisteria. This place is too Marcy—too perfect."

I realized a perfectionist would be a tough stepmother. "Do you have a mom somewhere?"

"She died from cancer when I was five. Dad and I did great for ten years, then he kind of went off the deep end."

"Meaning?"

"He fell in love."

I laughed out loud. "Love's the deep end?"

"You don't expect that to happen when your father is forty-eight. I mean, it was unbelievable. He acted like a teenager."

"I think it's awesome."

Obviously, Zack didn't. "Everything's different now."

"And you wanted things to stay the same, just you and him, even though you knew you'd be leaving for college one day."

Zack didn't answer right away, just pulled out his keys and opened the passenger door of his car. "Yeah, I'm selfish, if that's what you're getting at."

I got in, and he closed the door. I wondered if his dad had trained him to do these polite little things.

"I'm even worse," I said, when he got in on the other side. "I didn't want my mother to adopt Jack and the twins. I was going to be a freshman in high school. Everything was perfect—for me. I couldn't understand why she'd want to start all over again with little kids. Talk about acting like a princess!"

Zack looked at me for a long moment, then switched on the ignition. "And how about now?"

"Now I can't imagine life without them. I think I'm having SpongeBob withdrawal."

His eyes crinkled. I liked it when his smile made his eyes crinkle.

As we drove to the party, we talked about college and what we hoped it would be like. Finally, we turned into a lot with a sign that read SIMON'S WHARF. "Didn't we pass this place about fifteen minutes ago?" I asked, recognizing the bouquet of pink balloons attached to the sign.

"We did."

Zack did not explain why he had driven past the party, and I decided to pretend that all the guys I dated found me so fascinating that they drove past their destinations.

The pink "Happy 17th Birthday" balloons led us up a stairway to the second floor of the restaurant. Zack was carrying a square package wrapped in pink and gold.

"Was I supposed to bring a present?"

"I've got us covered," he said.

I wondered what he had selected and so thoughtfully wrapped in what appeared to be Erika's favorite color. In the restaurant pink roses wreathed a pink candle at the center of each table. Men in white jackets were setting up a long buffet with pink tapers and flowers. Close to the buffet sat a table of relatives—at least that's what they looked like: some middle-aged parental types, plus an old man and a youngish woman with a toddler. A DJ was working a soundboard close to a dance floor on the opposite side of the room from the relatives. Erika's friends were also staying as far from "the relatives" as possible.

At the center of the room was a table with a mound of gifts. I hoped we didn't have to sit and watch Erika open each one—she had invited maybe sixty of her closest friends.

"Let me get rid of this," Zack said, moving toward the pile. It reminded me of an altar, with a portrait-size photograph of Erika sitting on an easel in the center of the offerings.

As Zack placed his gift in the pile, I heard the girl next to me say, "I can't believe all the people she invited. I can't believe she invited *me*."

"Don't be naive," her friend replied. "Erika doesn't like us any more than she used to. She's scared, that's all. We weren't cool enough to be part of her game, and now she's afraid that somebody she snubbed is going to snitch. This is bribery, nothing else."

"It's expensive bribery."

"So? Daddy's paying for it."

"But does anybody who wasn't part of the game actually know enough to snitch? Does anyone have proof, anyone have a copy of the riddles she sent?"

At that point Zack returned. He smiled and said hello to the girls, then pulled me away from the information I had come for. I glanced back over my shoulder.

"Sorry. Did you want to talk to them?" he asked.

"No. No thanks." Not with him around.

"It will be cooler outside," he said.

The party had spilled onto a wide deck that faced the river. As Zack and I worked our way toward the deck, I became increasingly aware of people turning to look at me. I reminded myself I was in a town small enough for everyone to know everyone else; naturally, kids would notice a stranger. And maybe my arrival with Zack had given me celebrity status. Perhaps everyone was wondering what was going on, since it was Erika's party and she was obviously interested in him. My wry enjoyment of the moment ended abruptly, when I turned my head and met the gaze of my stalker. He smiled—if stretching your lips in a way that lacks any humor or friendliness can be called smiling.

"Let's get something to drink," Zack said, steering me away from him.

The guy next to the stalker whispered to his friend, then

said aloud, "That's got to be the old psycho's niece. Look at the hair."

A nervous titter followed his "accidentally" loud remark.

"Ignore him," Zack said quietly.

At that moment someone tapped me on my shoulder, and I turned around.

"Hi, I'm Erika." Without waiting for me to say hello, she slid between Zack and me, and, raising her arms, looped them around his neck. She kissed him on the mouth, lingering there longer than just-a-friend would. I watched the way her dark, silky hair fell straight down her long back until it brushed Zack's hands. When she turned to face me, she leaned back against him, just enough that he would have to be aware of her hair, her shoulders, her butt, and whatever else those things made him think of. I stared at her, not because of the way she had moved in and kissed him, but because I couldn't wrap my mind around the idea that three nights ago, while being invisible to her, with my body home in bed, I had looked at her face as closely as I was looking now.

"I'm Erika Gill. It's my birthday," she said, as if I didn't recognize her as the most important person there.

"Thanks for inviting me."

"Oh, it was Zack who invited you," she replied. "He likes you. He really likes you."

I nodded, careful not to look at him and trying hard not to get mad. "I get along with just about everybody."

"He keeps talking about you, so I said, 'Zack, just ask her, *ask* her.'"

Erika, who was wearing heels to die for, was taller than I by six inches and had the body of a model. She made a show of leaning down to whisper to me. "He can't take his eyes off of you."

I was ready to deny it, then got a better idea. Making a show of standing on my toes, I whispered back, "I know."

She stared down at me; I cheerfully smiled up her nose.

"Why don't you get her something to drink, Zack?" she said coolly, and moved on.

"So what would you like?" Zack asked, his voice neutral, as if he had not seen or heard any of what had just transpired between me and Erika. Guys can be so weird.

"Anything but spring water," I told him. "I just saw a tray of crab balls heading out to the deck. Do you want me to catch a few?"

"Sounds good," he said. "The drink line is long. I'll meet you back here."

I took my time getting to the waiter. It occurred to me that I might be spending the evening chasing down men with trays if I was to get myself free enough to eavesdrop.

My first two efforts turned up nothing but a lot of useless info about who was dating or cheating on whom. When Zack and I were on the outside deck, which under other circumstances would have been terribly romantic, and I went after the third tray of hors d'oeuvres, Zack said to me, "You know, we're getting dinner."

"I don't usually eat this late," I replied, and hurried off. Since there were plenty of girls willing to take my place with Zack, it wasn't that hard to escape.

For the last hour I had been secretly watching the stalker, who, when I had Zack by my side, was not as interested in me. I had just caught the look he had sent to a guy across the deck, the slight flick of the head, and the catlike way he moved toward a railing as if he didn't want anyone to notice him, before he dropped out of sight—down a set of steps, I realized. A minute later the guy across the deck headed for the same stairs. Then I did. I had no idea what I was going to do if they turned and confronted me. Jump in the river, maybe.

I took off my heels at the top of the wooden steps so they wouldn't click. Halfway down to the first level, I was relieved to see there were people sitting on the lower deck, and beyond glass doors there was a dining room. My eyes swept the deck. I positioned myself behind a waiter's station and looked more carefully a second time. The guys must have gone inside.

The Back Door of Midnight

The doors and windows on the first floor of the restaurant were closed, which meant I'd call attention to myself entering the dining room from the deck side. I walked to the end of the deck, climbed over the railing, and jumped three feet down to the lot below. After slipping my heels back on, I headed for the restaurant's main entrance and followed a group of diners inside, a man and woman with little kids who kept poking each other. Standing behind them at the hostess desk, I saw my stalker and his friend in a booth against a wall. The wall was about four feet tall and decorated with bushel baskets and nets, orange crabs climbing all over them, which looked dumb because crabs are blue when they're still able to move. But I was grateful for the decor, especially when I saw that a hallway to the restrooms ran behind that wall.

"May I help you?" the suntanned hostess asked me.

"Where is your ladies' room?"

She pointed to the hallway.

"Thanks."

I hurried toward it, ducked inside, removed one of my earrings, then returned to the little hall. No one was watching, so I dropped the earring close to where I thought the booth was. There I knelt, ready to act as if I were searching for it if someone came by.

Having gone to all that trouble, I discovered the stalker and his friend were talking about music. I was just about to give up when I heard one of them say to the other, "You're so uptight. What's wrong with you?"

"She hasn't found her cell phone."

"She hasn't?" There was a long silence, then the same guy spoke again. "Well, it's been a week. If the police or firefighters found it and figured out it was Erika's, they'd have contacted her by now. It's no big deal. . . . She pulled her SIM card, right?"

"Wrong."

"She didn't?!"

"She didn't know she dropped the phone."

The other guy swore.

"I told Erika to delete every message in her account, but if the police have already gotten into it, we're all going down together."

There was another silence.

"Does she use a password?"

"Yeah, but they can crack that."

"McManus?" The guy snickered. "Not likely."

"They sent the old man's body to Baltimore. They probably sent everything they had."

"The video. She used her phone to take video of the fires and to shoot pictures of kids arriving."

At that moment an older woman started toward me. "Did you lose something, dear?"

In response, I lifted up my shiny earring. When the woman moved on, I crawled a few feet past the booth, then stood up and headed toward the stairs.

Friends shared phones, I thought; close friends shared passwords. Who would be the most likely person to know Erika's— and how could I wheedle it out of him?

Fifteen

"WHERE WERE YOU?" Zack asked. "I looked indoors and out. You just disappeared."

"The ladies' room." The only way for me to lie effectively was by telling the truth—at least, half a truth.

"I thought you were chasing down scallops wrapped in bacon." The laughter I'd seen earlier in his eyes had disappeared.

"I couldn't catch up with the tray. Looks like dinner is being served. I'm starved."

Zack's frown told me he didn't buy my excuses.

Good. You don't trust me, and I don't trust you, I thought, but it bothered me the way the light in his eyes had changed. We went through the buffet line silently, then sat with three other couples at a round table. I found myself talking to the girl and guy next to me and avoiding conversation with Zack. When I surveyed the room, I didn't see the stalker or his friend.

Dinner was begun with a toast by Mr. Gill. Waiters had

scurried around filling champagne glasses with bubbly fruit juice, then he stood up and asked us to raise our glasses in honor of the most beautiful seventeen-year-old in the world, the most wonderful of daughters, the best friend any of us could ever have, et cetera, et cetera.

The girl next to me whispered, "I'm glad this is before dinner. I'd hate to puke," which made me snort my sip of bubbly stuff, drawing an unreadable look from Zack. It may have been the longest toast and the longest dinner I have ever endured.

Like a wedding reception, cake was going to be served much later. Erika invited us all to dance and told the guys that she expected one dance with each of them. Otherwise, it was a lot like any other event with music: girls dancing with girls, since the guys weren't enthusiastic about it.

"Want to go out on the deck?" Zack asked.

"Okay."

We had almost reached the door when Erika caught up with us. "You owe me a dance, Zack. And because you tried to escape, you owe me several."

Zack smiled. "Let me know when you're ready."

"I'm ready now."

"I'll be outside," I said.

Zack nodded and walked with Erika to the dance floor. It was a prime opportunity for me to float around and latch on to a conversation that would provide further information. But my feet stayed planted on the deck close to the doorway. I really didn't want to, but like the other girls, I watched.

Erika was a video tutorial on seductive dance. Lesson 1: When the song is fast and everyone's jumping around, dance as if the music is slow; it makes you and the guy seem like you are in a romantic world all your own. Lesson 2: Take off your shoes; drop back your head to gaze into the guy's eyes, making him feel taller and making your hair longer, so it hangs down your back and touches his fingers. Lesson 3: Loop your hands around his neck, pretending to be casual and easy, then use your fingertips to touch and tantalize. Lesson 4—

"It was the 'green tunnel' that I got," said a girl behind me.

I turned my head and missed Lesson 4.

"Erika makes the early clues impossible," a guy replied. "'Turn at the spring flower'? I didn't even know there was a thing called a tulip tree."

Tulip poplar, I thought. The tree that marked the road that ran through Tilby's Dream.

"I didn't either," the girl admitted, "but my little brother calls tree-shaded streets 'tunnels.' When we got that clue, I could picture it. And then, when Erika sent out 'Farmer's dream—'"

"Everyone got it then. This time, everyone beat the fire trucks."

The pair moved past me, through the door and toward the dance floor.

I walked slowly to the edge of the deck and leaned on the wood railing, gazing out at the river, trying to piece things together. There was a game of riddles, starting with the more cryptic clues, hinting where the fire would be set. Maybe the point was to text the riddle's answer to Erika, then get to the site in time to watch her set the fire. Even if Erika deleted the incriminating texts from her account, the experts could retrieve them as well as the video of the fire. I had the evidence the police needed but, unfortunately, not the information and explanations that I wanted.

I really disliked Erika, but I had trouble imagining she knew that Uncle Will was in the trunk of the car. She was a party girl. Her goals in life were guys, clothes, and lots of attention. But she wouldn't want the kind of attention you get with a corpse; and for her, an old man wouldn't matter enough to bother with—unless he was seriously cramping her style. Maybe he had seen something and threatened to turn her in. Or maybe it was just bad luck that she had ended up with a charred body. Or maybe, someone who had an issue with Uncle Will and a real streak of violence had taken advantage of the situation. I wondered how many contacts were on Erika's e-mail list. I wondered if Aunt Iris could "sense" that kind of stuff.

"Thinking about taking a swim?"

I turned quickly, then turned back, facing the river; I hadn't heard Zack's footsteps approaching from behind. "Not at night," I said.

"Why not? I love swimming at night."

"Dark water is scary. You can't see what lies beneath its surface."

"But that's what I like about it," he replied. "It's mysterious."

"And dangerous," I told him. "Nothing changes as much as water."

"That's my *favorite* thing about it."

"At night the harbor in Baltimore is beautiful with all the city and dock lights reflected in it, but the reflections keep you from seeing the water itself."

"If you are painting it, Anna, the reflections *are* the water."

I turned to him. "But if you fall in, they're *not*."

He took my face in his hands and looked into my eyes; I felt as if I had slipped off a bank and was drowning in his gaze. I looked away.

"Do you want to dance?" he asked softly.

"It's hot in there."

"Out here," he suggested.

"Most guys I know don't like to dance."

"Most guys *I* know want to dance, if it's with the right girl."

"Oops. Song's over." And it really was. But the music started again, with a slower beat.

"Come on, Anna. Why do you make things so hard?"

"Maybe you expect things to be too easy."

He laughed and put his arms loosely around my waist. "Come on."

I kept my heels on, and I looped my hands around his neck. I didn't try Erika's touch-and-tantalize strategy, partly because I didn't think I could pull it off, mostly because just feeling his arms around me was enough touching and tantalizing.

As we danced, Zack pulled me closer. I couldn't see his face now. I thought—maybe I was wrong—I thought he spoke my name, as if he had said it silently but I heard it anyway. Then I felt his hand on the back of my neck. He leaned my head against his chest. I could hear his heart beating. In half a breath I could have raised my face to kiss him. I felt him lowering his head. In half a breath—

I got a bucket of cold reality. Through the door to the dining room, I saw Erika standing next to the DJ, watching us, her arms crossed, a satisfied smile on her lips. Zack was on assignment.

I pulled back. Zack stopped dancing. "What is it?" He gently touched my face, lifting my chin with just the backs of his fingers. I gazed into eyes the color of the creek at twilight. I don't know what Zack saw in my gaze, but he quickly let go of my face and started dancing again, as if he were afraid to look any longer.

He ought to be afraid, I thought. *His conscience ought to be cowering in the basement of his brain. Faker!*

"Do you remember Monday night?" I asked.

"Monday . . ."

"Do you remember what you said?"

He shook his head no.

"Well, you were right."

"I was right?" he repeated. "About—?"

"You can fake it with anyone."

He took a step back, staring at me as if I had just slapped him.

I turned, headed for the dining room, and moved quickly through it, using the crowd to make it hard for Zack to catch up. I hurried down the staircase. When I got to the first floor, all I wanted to do was run to the bathroom and bawl. I stood still in the hallway that led to the ladies' room and shut my eyes, trying to keep the tears from slipping out. I was such a sucker!

"Are you all right? Are you all right?" a man asked.

I opened my eyes. Mr. Gill.

"You look very upset," he said, his voice sympathetic.

"I'm fine."

He kept staring at me. "I saw you hurrying across the dance floor. I feared that something was wrong."

"Nothing's wrong."

He shook his head slightly. "You're a friend of my daughter, but I don't know your name."

At first I thought it was kindness—unwanted kindness—and I tried to think of a polite way to tell him to get lost. Then I realized why he was so concerned and why he had followed me down the stairs. He knew my name—the name I was born with—and I knew his old phone number. "Anna O'Neill Kirkpatrick," I replied, and watched Elliot Gill swallow hard.

"I'm not really friends with Erika. I arrived in Wisteria just a few days ago. I came tonight with Zack, who lives next door to my great-aunt."

"Of course," he said. "You came because of your uncle's death."

I explained once again how I had been responding to Uncle Will's invitation and didn't learn he was dead until I arrived. Elliot Gill never took his eyes off me. The way he listened, his mouth moving as if he were anticipating my words, as if thirsty for whatever I had to say, made me wonder if I not only looked like my mother, but sounded like her.

"Your aunt Iris," he said, "how is she taking all this?"

"The way anyone who knows her would expect. She still talks to Uncle Will."

"Crazy as a loon," he remarked softly.

"Maybe."

Mr. Gill raised a pale eyebrow. His eyes were gray, his hair a thin mix of gray and yellow combed across the large dome of his head. Erika must have gotten her dark beauty from her mother.

He pointed to a booth, the one where the stalker and his friend had sat. "Why don't we sit and chat?"

I wanted to go home and cry my eyes out, but I pulled myself together. One of my reasons for coming to this stupid party was to ask him questions about my mother.

As soon as I slid into the private, candlelit booth, I wished I had insisted on a table in the center of the room. It was the way he looked at me. I wanted to keep reminding him, *I'm Anna! Anna!*

"You're not staying with Iris, I hope?"

"What do you mean?"

"You should stay with me," he said. "We have an extra room next to Erika's. You will be safe with me."

"Thank you, but I really like being with Aunt Iris."

"Are you aware of the degree to which Iris suffers from mental illness?"

"I've never seen her medical records, but I have some idea."

"Over the years she has been in and out of hospitals. As you may or may not know, your mother's life with Iris and William was extremely difficult."

"It would have been more difficult without them," I replied, feeling the need to defend them. "It would have been hard for my mother to keep me and continue with school."

"She had options."

"She did? Like what?"

He didn't answer.

"You mean there were other people she could have lived with."

"Exactly."

"What was Joanna like?" I asked.

He stared at the flickering candle. It took him a long time to answer. "Bright, imaginative, beautiful. . . . She was a young woman with big dreams. I had just purchased my first store— I'm a pharmacist by training—and hired her to work part-time behind the counter. Joanna was hoping to attend medical school, but after she became pregnant, she thought nursing a more practical choice. She was a healer by nature, intuitive about people."

"She was psychic," I said.

He went on as if he hadn't heard me, his narrow fingers

tracing a pattern on the tabletop. "She was so innocent, so full of life. I watched her fall in love." His eyes rose to meet mine. "When a young woman falls in love, she looks a certain way, has a certain light in her face. She becomes irresistible."

I folded my arms and sat as far back as I could.

"You move like your mother," he said.

I unfolded my arms, as if I could undo that observation.

"You have the same eyes and hair. Joanna often wore red."

"I don't."

"She loved reds and pinks," he continued. "Of course, everyone told her she should wear green or blue. She wore red defiantly."

I smiled. "Then we share that—defiance."

"You should try those colors, perhaps just a pretty pink or red scarf. She loved to wear scarves. She loved anything that floated."

I was glad Mrs. Gill wasn't around to hear the tone in his voice. "Are you my father?"

"God above! No."

"It seemed a reasonable thing to ask."

"Joanna wouldn't tell me or anyone else who your father was. He lived on the West Coast, traveled for work, and spent a lot of time on the East Coast—I know that much. He was married and didn't tell her, not until she got pregnant."

"Then left her high and dry—nice of him."

"She had options," he replied.

"Why do you keep saying that?"

"I offered to marry her and accept you as my child."

"Oh!"

I tried to imagine it, living with this man in a manse on the river, wearing designer clothes, carrying the most expensive phone, driving a car that people envied. . . . I thought about it and decided that, if the choice had been mine, I would have preferred Joanna to shack up with Mom in our Baltimore town house. "Okay, I see now. Joanna said no."

"William said no!"

"But it was her choice, wasn't it?"

"Precisely," he said, not understanding what I meant.

It seemed to me that if my mother had been anything like me—if she had been the kind to wear red defiantly—she would not have let Uncle Will dictate that decision. Maybe Mr. Gill just couldn't admit she had rejected him.

He talked as if he were still in love with her. Her rejection must have hurt him deeply and made him angry. Erika had just turned seventeen, meaning she was eleven months younger than I. My mother had said no, and Elliot Gill had married someone else soon after.

"If Joanna had married me, she would be alive today."

I glanced up. "Excuse me?"

He shifted uncomfortably. "She wouldn't have been living in that wretched house when the place was robbed."

There was a long silence between us. How angry was he? I wondered. Aloud I asked, "What do you think Uncle Will wanted to tell me about my mother?"

"I have no idea. We weren't on speaking terms." His hands were tightly clasped. The tips of his fingers twitched, then he said in a gentler tone, "I suppose he wanted to tell you what she was like. . . . I would very much like to see you with your hair up. You should wear a scarf—"

"I don't have any scarves."

"I'll buy you one."

I'd heard enough and started sliding out of the booth. As I was standing up, a woman with Erika's hair and eyes, and Erika's unfriendly expression, walked toward us.

"Elliot," she said, "we are waiting for you."

"My love, this is Anna O'Neill."

She ignored me. "Erika wants to open her gifts."

"Of course." He rose to his feet, gesturing for me to join them.

"I'll be up in a minute," I said, and headed toward the ladies' room. Before I had gotten to its door, they disappeared, and I left the restaurant.

Sixteen

ON THE OTHER side of the bridge, Scarborough Road became a country road with no streetlamps. When leaving the restaurant, I hadn't thought about the fact that walking home at 10:45 at night meant finding my way down an overgrown driveway without the aid of headlights. At the entrance to the drive, the moon silvered the edges of the high grass and weeds, making it bright enough to see. But when I reached the trees, their dense foliage suffocated the light, and the humidity and darkness closed in around me. As I walked, I couldn't shake the feeling that someone was hidden in the trees, watching me.

I heard a rustling sound, like a person brushing against leaves, and I stopped, turning my head slightly. The sound had come from somewhere ahead of me and to the right. Reluctant to go on, I looked over my shoulder, but I was already too far down the driveway—I couldn't discern a clearing either behind or ahead of me. I took two more steps. Again I heard the sound, this time directly to the right. *Cats,* I told myself. *The cats are out hunting.* Sweat trickled down my neck. I moved quickly, hoping to get past whatever it was.

Reaching the front door, I found it unlocked as usual. I hurried inside, closed the door, and leaned back against it. Then it occurred to me: Someone else could have done the same—the house was no safer than the woods. I felt for the wall switch, flicked on the hall light, and glanced around.

"Is that you?" Aunt Iris called from upstairs.

I let out my breath in relief. "Yes. It's Anna. I'm home from the party. Sorry I woke you up."

"You didn't." She sounded as if she were standing directly above me, in the hall outside her bedroom. "I just got home myself."

"Aunt Iris, would you mind if I locked the door tonight?"

"The front door? Not at all, as long as you keep the kitchen door open."

"I meant all the doors."

"No, don't do that," she called down. "I lost my key."

"Well, how about if we lock the house just during the night?"

"No, I lost my key."

I sighed. "Okay. Remind me to look for it tomorrow."

"Five years ago," she said.

I told myself that it didn't really matter. It was impossible to make the house secure; the old screens and windows could be worked open by a child. I checked the charge on my cell phone, then climbed the steps to the second floor. I heard my aunt scurry into her bedroom and shut the door, as if afraid I'd catch a glimpse of her.

"Is everything okay?" I asked, reaching the hall.

"Yes," she called from behind her door.

I walked toward her room. "Can I get you something before I go to bed?"

"No. No, I'm perfectly well."

"May I open your door?"

"Please don't."

I hesitated.

"I just need a little rest," she said.

I gave in. Everyone needs privacy. Besides, with no mirror left to break, she might launch a missile at me. "Okay. Good night."

When I reached my room, I turned on the fan, snatched up my nightshirt, and headed back down the hall to the bathroom. A long, lukewarm shower cooled me. I was rubbing my hair dry when I heard the phone ringing downstairs.

It hadn't rung since I had been there, and it sounded loud and foreboding.

"If it's William," Aunt Iris called from her bedroom, "I can't speak to him now."

That made me laugh, and I ran downstairs to get it. "Hello?"

"You're home."

Zack.

"I'm home," I said stiffly.

"You left without telling me."

"I thought it was pretty obvious."

"You were rude."

"Really!" I said. "Well, let me tell you what I think is rude. It's using a girl. It's acting like you want to be friends when all you want is information. It's going along with another girl's plan, because *you* can fake it with anyone."

There was a long silence. "How do you know that?" he asked at last.

"I just do," I said, and hung up.

Anger is better than fear, I told myself as I climbed the steps again. But it was anger and hurt that I felt. I combed out my hair, yanking on a knot. *Get over it, Anna.*

It was a relief to return to my little corner in the attic, where I had once felt so safe. Then I saw the books.

At first I didn't know what bothered me about them. They

were on the floor next to my bed, where I had left them the other night. I stretched out as I had when reading and reached down to them, resting my fingers on the top of the pile. The angle was wrong; it would have been awkward for me to set the books down that way. But it would have been quite natural if I had stood facing the bed. Had someone picked them up, looked at them, then carelessly put them back?

I glanced around the room, then walked over to my bureau. When I opened the top drawer, everything in it looked the same. Still, my fingertips tingled, as if they sensed the touch of hands other than mine. *So Aunt Iris got a little curious,* I told myself. I had peeked in her room; why shouldn't she look in mine?

As logical as that was, I couldn't sleep until I checked the rooms below. Not wanting to disturb my aunt, I crossed the attic to the stairs that led down to Uncle Will's den. As soon as I turned on his desk lamp, I saw that someone had been there. I knew I had closed the drawers tightly, not wanting Aunt Iris to know I had been snooping. Someone else had been careless or rushed. I checked behind the books where I had hidden my mother's client book. It was still there. I hurried upstairs and unzipped the front pocket of my suitcase. The cell phone was missing. My evidence against Erika and her friends was gone. I checked the large pocket again: so was Uncle Will's letter to the police and the article about my mother's death. Why?

If Aunt Iris had been the one searching, she might have found the phone and realized it was the one she had picked up at the fire site. She had buried it the first time and may have wanted to do it again, for whatever crazy reason. But why would she take the letter and article? Maybe she thought she could keep me from asking questions and opening old wounds. Or maybe she didn't have time to look at the contents and, seeing that the envelope was from Uncle Will and addressed to the state police, imagined that Uncle Will was "reporting" her to them. Her broken mirror had proven just how paranoid she was.

There was another possibility. Everyone who had seen me at Erika's party would have counted on me staying at the restaurant for several hours. I hadn't seen the stalker at dinner. Had I made him nervous enough to check out my things? If the stalker was one of the kids who'd harassed Uncle Will, he might have seen the state police address on the missing envelope and assumed the contents implicated him.

My skin crept at the memory of walking down the dark driveway and hearing something—someone—moving through the trees. I turned out the light, then went from window to window, peering out of all six windows of the attic and those in

my mother's room as well. The words I had heard the night of
the fire floated back to me: *Anna, be careful.*

Careful of what, Uncle Will? Careful of whom?

Next morning, with the sun back up, I was ready to take on
everybody. I ate breakfast quickly, listening for my aunt's footsteps. Her bedroom door had been closed when I got up and
her car was parked outside, so I assumed she was home. After
breakfast I went upstairs to check on her.

"Aunt Iris?" I called, knocking softly on the door. I called
a second time, more loudly, and finally banged hard. I heard
movement within the room, a creaking of floorboards. It
sounded as if she had been standing at the door the entire time
I was knocking.

"It's Anna. Would you open the door, please?"

"I'd rather not."

"I'm going to work. Before I leave, I'd like to see you."

She didn't reply. Last night I had respected her privacy, but
I didn't think it smart to let her isolate herself for this amount
of time, especially since someone other than she may have been
searching the house.

"I am going to open your door," I warned her.

"You can try, but it's locked."

I did, and it was. "Aunt Iris, when I got home last night, it looked as if someone had searched my room and Uncle Will's study."

She didn't make a sound. It frustrated me that, unable to see her face, I couldn't tell if this was news to her. "Was anyone else here last night?"

"I don't remember."

"There was a cell phone in my room, in my suitcase. It's gone."

"It wasn't yours," she said.

"Where is it now?"

"I don't remember."

"There was a newspaper article about my mother's death and a draft of a letter to the police, asking for information about it. Did you take them?"

She didn't answer.

"Somebody did," I said.

"I'm glad they're gone. William was being foolish."

So she knew about the documents. "I want them back."

"The past is the past. I tried to tell William that. He wouldn't listen to me. We can do nothing about the past."

"We can understand it!"

I strode down the hall to the room with the blue-flowered wallpaper. It was time for me to face the contents of the mahogany bureau, to learn whatever I could from the bits and pieces left behind by my mother.

I entered the room and, after a moment of hesitation, slid open the small top drawer of the bureau. Combs, hair fasteners, and several pairs of earrings—simple, inexpensive ones, like the kind I would buy—lay with a note written in my uncle's hand: *These are for Anna.* I liked the necklace next to them, a chain with a pendant. I touched it gently, then held it up to the window light, admiring its clear golden drop—amber, I thought. I fastened it around my neck and felt the way it rested against my chest, as if it belonged to and had been waiting for me.

I opened the next drawer and found underwear, ordinary stuff. In the next were T-shirts. I held them up to me, wondering if my mother and I were the same size; we were. In the next drawer I discovered jeans. Straightening up, I held them against me. Yup.

I opened the last drawer. It was filled with scarves—red, pink, purple—some plain, some with geometric shapes. I picked up a filmy pink one and draped it around my neck. Footsteps sounded in the hall, and I turned quickly to see Aunt Iris standing in the doorway. She cocked her head to one side, studying me, then stepped into the room.

"You would look so much better, Joanna, with your hair out of your face."

Anna, I was about to say, then caught myself. Maybe, if I pretended to be Joanna, she would talk as if we were in the past and tell me things I needed to know. I opened the top drawer again, picked up a comb and an elastic band, and pulled my hair up on my head.

"Better, much better," she said, "but don't let it hang like a horse's tail."

I twisted my hair into a bun and pinned it in place, feeling a little creepy, knowing that this was what Mr. Gill had wanted me to do.

She nodded approvingly.

I tried to think of something to talk about that would seem natural coming from Joanna. "I have appointments with two clients today."

She sighed. "We have plenty of money. You should focus on your studies."

"But you have clients," I argued.

"Mine can be trusted," she replied. "It's *yours* that bite."

I laughed, trying to be agreeable. "I like helping people, the same way you like helping animals."

"You must be careful whom you help," she said. "Forget about Mick."

"Mick?" I asked.

"Let go of the past. It's over now. Nothing can be done."

"Mick?" I repeated.

Her eyes sparked. "Stop pretending, Joanna! I know what you're up to!"

I wondered if Mick were my father. "You mean my . . . my lover," I said tentatively.

She looked stunned. "*Your* lover?"

"Well, who else's?" I replied, frustrated.

My aunt shook her head. "You should have married Elliot Gill when you had the chance. He would have provided for you and Anna."

"Because he is Anna's father," I responded, not trusting what Mr. Gill had told me last night.

My aunt took a step back. "He is? That's not what you told me."

I played with my scarf, afraid that if I said much more, she would realize I wasn't Joanna.

"You said he was from California," Aunt Iris went on. "You said he lied about himself, gave you a false name, and never told you he was married."

Their stories matched. "That's right," I replied. "I was joking about Elliot. But I can't stop thinking about Mick," I added, hoping she would explain why she wanted Joanna to forget him.

She said nothing more, but I had observed her response, the way she flinched at his name. As soon as possible, I would check my mother's appointment book to see if I could find a reference to him, although the initial *M* began a lot of common names.

Maybe Erika's father would know who Mick was. I would call him at work.

Work! "Oh no, I'm going to be late!" I said, dropping the scarf on the bureau and rushing past Aunt Iris. I grabbed my purse from my room and dashed to my car. Flying up the rutted driveway, I sent cats racing in all directions.

Seventeen

"NEW HAIRSTYLE, VERY professional," Marcy observed when I entered the shop that morning.

"It's cooler this way."

"It's perfect with that necklace, pretty and professional. The fact is, people like pretty women and pretty things, and it's foolish for a businesswoman not to use those assets."

"I guess."

She laughed her tinkly laugh and turned back to the display she was creating.

The shop was busy through lunchtime, then the crowd dwindled at the usual hour—three o'clock. Marcy gave me a list of names and addresses to enter into the store's computerized database while she worked on her laptop. We drifted in and out of conversation, and I kept waiting for her to bring up last night's "date." To my relief, she didn't.

At three thirty she rose to stretch, then glanced out the

front window. "I was wondering when he'd show up."

"Who?"

"I've been biting my tongue," Marcy admitted, "trying not to ask how it went last night."

"The party was nice."

She lowered her head to look at me over her reading glasses. "Zack was not exactly his charming, cheerful self this morning."

I nodded but said nothing.

"I'll stay out of it," she said. "Given my track record before I met Dave, the last thing you want from me is romantic advice."

She returned to her computer, and I retyped a misspelled address—three times. Zack entered the shop.

"Hi."

"Hi."

If the normal "hi" were sung the length of a half note, we held ours for just a sixteenth.

"Hello, Zack," Marcy said. "How is everything with your father?"

"Fine. I was hoping to talk to Anna. Can she take a break?"

"She has earned one," Marcy replied, "but it's up to her if she wants to take it now."

Zack turned to me. "We need to talk."

"I'm listening."

"I mean outside."

I glanced at Marcy. She had walked behind Zack, pretending to be adjusting something on a shelf, but turned her head toward me and gave a slight nod.

"All right," I said, saving my work.

I led the way out of the shop and stopped when we reached the brick sidewalk.

"Away from the shop," Zack directed, then added with less certainty, "Okay?"

"Okay."

We walked all the way down to the river. I would have cracked a joke about how acute Marcy's hearing was, but I wasn't going to be the one to start the conversation. We reached the public landing, a square wharf that had benches for sitting and pilings for temporary docking. On this hot, sticky day it was deserted. Two sailboats rested motionless on the Sycamore, pinned to a sullen sky.

"You were at the fire site the other night," he said.

I didn't reply.

"I was careful," he went on. "I made sure no one followed us. But you were there."

What was I supposed to say? Part of me was there, but my body was home in bed.

"You got there before Erika and I did."

He searched my face, looking for answers. He must have realized that, standing in the clearing, he would have seen anyone close enough to hear their conversation.

"Maybe I'm psychic," I said. "Or maybe I'm just a good guesser. It doesn't make any difference. The fact is, when you asked me out, you were using me."

"If you were really psychic, you'd know better!"

"Erika told you to dance with me. You were following instructions."

"Sometimes girls do that, tell a guy to dance with another girl. Girls like to play matchmaker."

"Matchmaker! Then Erika needs to work on her skills. Most guys aren't attracted to 'freckled little carrots.'"

Zack flushed and muttered two swear words, for which I was grateful. It made me laugh. I'm sure he had no idea how close I was to tears.

"Anna, listen," he said. "Things are complicated. Erika did some really stupid stuff. She broke the law, but she didn't kill your uncle. She told me she torched the inside of the car, the seats, but she never opened the trunk. She had no idea his body was in there. She thinks someone framed her. She's scared and trying to figure out who's behind it. The thing you have to remember is that she hasn't done anything to hurt you personally."

"She could do a lot more to help," I replied. "Hasn't it

occurred to you that the person who put my uncle's body in the trunk could have known about Erika's game? She needs to go to the police and give them the list of people she texts. One of those kids or someone who has access to their phone or e-mail accounts might have seen the arson as a perfect opportunity for covering a murder."

He nodded. "I've thought of that, and I've been trying to get her to do it. She's afraid if she does, she will get everyone else in trouble."

"Oh, spare me!" I said. "Erika's a self-centered drama queen, worried about nobody but herself. Anyway, *you* could go to the sheriff. Why don't you send McManus a copy of her list?"

"I don't have it."

"Just type the stupid names!" I exploded. "Don't act so helpless. Make a list of the people you've seen at the fires."

"I've never gone."

I stared at him. "What?" I couldn't believe it. "Are you crazy? Why would you even try to help—?"

"She's a friend."

"Well, then, you've got lousy taste in friends."

We stood a foot apart, staring at each other. Zack turned away first and sat on a bench facing the water, resting his forearms on his knees. I began to pace.

"Someone searched my room last night."

He straightened up. "When?"

"While I was at the party. Searched my room and Uncle Will's den."

"How do you know that?" he asked.

"The searcher wasn't very careful."

"Was anything taken?"

"Erika's cell phone."

"You have her cell phone?" he asked, surprised.

"Not anymore." I continued to pace from one side of the landing to the other.

"Where did you find it?"

"Aunt Iris found it, at the fire site, I guess. She buried it in the backyard with what she believes are Uncle Will's ashes, which I got curious about and dug up. By the way, what is the name of Wisteria's friendly neighborhood stalker?"

"Carl. Carl Wiedefeld. Why?"

"I didn't see him while we were eating dinner. He may have left the restaurant."

"Was anything else taken?" Zack caught my arm as I passed. "Anna, would you stand still?" He reached for my other hand and pulled me around the bench. "Please sit," he said. "Is your aunt okay?"

"Meaning is she the same as before—a crazy-but-still-functioning kind of okay? As far as I can tell."

"And you're okay?"

I looked away. "Of course."

"Was anything else taken?" He was talking in that gentle voice he used with Erika: I guess I was his friend too. It was a good thing I wasn't skilled enough to cry and look beautiful; I might have been tempted to pull "an Erika." But this was just a passing moment of weakness.

"A news article and a letter my uncle had planned to send to the state police."

Zack was quiet for a moment. "Why the state police rather than the sheriff? What was it about?"

"The death of my mother."

He frowned. "I thought that was a long time ago. Marcy said she died when you were a baby."

"I was three." The humid river air had made it impossible for sweat to evaporate, and an unexpected breeze gave my damp skin goose bumps. I rubbed my arms like a person with fever and chills. Zack laid his hand on my back for a moment, then shifted his position as if uncertain that I wanted to be touched.

"How did she die?" he asked quietly.

"In a robbery. The police believe she surprised the intruder. It was a blow to the head. I read it in the article that was taken from my room."

"The sheriff said your uncle was struck on the head."

Two people from the same family killed in the same way—I had avoided making that connection as long as possible, reluctant to connect the dots to Aunt Iris's inclination to smash things when she was angry. Had Uncle Will questioned the theory about my mother's death? Was his murder a successful effort to silence him? My imagination was running away with me!

"Anna, be careful," Zack said.

"Careful of whom?" I asked. "Aunt Iris? Carl? How about Erika's father?"

"Her father?"

"He wanted to marry my mother—Joanna—and he blames Uncle Will for coming between them. I look like her. Aunt Iris keeps talking to me as if I'm her. Last night the way Mr. Gill looked at me creeped me out. He told me he'd like to see me wearing the colors Joanna wore. He wanted to buy me a scarf, the kind that she liked."

Zack shook his head. "I don't know what to think."

"That makes two of us." I glanced at my watch. "I should get back to work."

He stood up with me. "I'll walk you there."

"Please don't."

He pressed his lips together.

"It's just that I—I need a few minutes by myself."

He studied my face, then nodded. I left him staring at the river.

I was grateful to Marcy for biting her tongue a second time that day. When I returned to the shop, she looked at me curiously but refrained from asking questions. Before leaving work on Friday, I looked up pharmacies in a county phone book. Mr. Gill owned four, which would make it harder to locate him away from home, but I had to talk to him again, and I didn't want to do it around his wife or Erika. I had to find out who Mick was.

The closest pharmacy listed was on the corner of Scarborough and Crown, which was just one block over from High Street. I drove the short distance, parked behind the store, and went in to ask about Mr. Gill's schedule.

Our pharmacy in Baltimore is in the back of a 24/7 grocery store with bright aisles, piped-in baby-boomer music, and great smells wafting in from its deli and bakery. This place was silent. It smelled like Vicks VapoRub and plastic. The boxes of candy, wrapped in cellophane, looked as if they had been sitting next to the canes and commodes since my mother worked there.

"May I help you?"

The woman behind the prescription counter listened to my

request and was copying down my name and cell phone number on a message pad when I saw a venetian blind flip in the office behind her. Reflections off the glass made it hard to see in, but a moment later the office door opened, and Mr. Gill emerged.

He smiled at me. "Anna. You've come."

I tried not to squirm at the warmth in his voice. "Yes, I have a question."

"It's wonderful to see you."

"Thanks. This won't take long."

"Should I lock up now, Mr. Gill?" the woman asked.

He nodded. "Thank you, Myrtle."

"Oh. Oh, sorry," I said quickly. "I didn't realize it was closing time. I'll come back when you're open."

Being alone with him in the store would be even creepier than chatting in the restaurant booth. He had probably enjoyed being alone here with my mother.

"No, no. I'm happy to answer your questions. Come into my office."

I hesitated, then told myself to stop being paranoid. When I entered the small room, I chose the chair that was close to the office door rather than the one he gestured to.

"You've worn your hair up," he said. "You look lovely."

"Thanks. I would like to know—"

"The pendant. It's quite perfect on you."

My hand went up to my chest, touching the teardrop of amber that I had taken from Joanna's bureau that morning. Did he think I was dressing like her to please him?

"I gave it to her," he said.

"Oh. . . . Oh, I see." I reached for the necklace's latch. "Do you want it back?"

"No. I enjoy seeing it on you."

Well, I no longer enjoyed wearing it, and no amount of small talk was going to make me comfortable with him. I cut to the chase. "Who's Mick?"

"Mick," he repeated softly. "Mick Sanchez. He didn't mean to cause any trouble. All he did was die. How has his name come up?"

I told Mr. Gill what little I knew.

He nodded. "Mick Sanchez was married to Audrey. They worked for the Fairfaxes, whose home—one of their homes—is on Oyster Creek. You may have seen it."

"Next to the Flemings'," I said. "Marcy was a Fairfax."

"That's right. Perhaps you have already met Audrey, who works for Marcy now."

"Yes. So why was my mother supposed to forget about Audrey's husband?"

"He died suddenly, several months before Joanna. Audrey

held your mother responsible for his death. I suppose that Iris was telling Joanna to forget about all that."

"All what?" I did the math, subtracting fifteen years from Audrey's current age. "He must have been a lot older than my mother. They weren't having an affair, were they?"

"Lord, no."

"How did he die?"

"In a car accident, on Scarborough Road, I believe, a few miles after it crosses Wist Creek."

"Did my mother cause it? Did she run into him?"

"No, she simply didn't foresee it. Audrey was a frequent client of Joanna's and—"

"A *client* of my mother's?" I interrupted. "But Audrey thinks psychics are tools of the devil. She thinks all of us O'Neills are going straight to hell."

"Now she does. At that time, however, she was your mother's steadiest customer—she was dependent on her, really, couldn't do anything without first consulting Joanna. She asked for readings so often, Joanna felt uneasy. But when her husband was killed, Audrey turned on your mother. She blamed her for not foreseeing Mick's accident, for not warning them."

"That's crazy," I said. "I understand wanting to blame someone at first—you're upset and everything—but eventually, you think clearly again. Anyway, I can't understand how Audrey could have changed that much."

"In essence, she didn't," he replied. "She simply exchanged one extreme belief for another. Audrey is the kind of person who can't stand feeling uncertain about things. People like her feel safer when they latch on to something that makes them feel like they've got the answer, makes them feel like they're in control. The first way let her down, so now she is trying another."

"Did my mother blame herself?"

"She felt very bad about Mick's death. She felt Audrey's anger and pain, felt it keenly."

How angry was Audrey Sanchez? Angry enough to kill? But how could someone so religious justify that?

The theory I had spun for Aunt Iris could be applied to Audrey: Angry, she had struck my mother, never intending to kill her. Afterward, she had panicked and ransacked the house to make it look like a robbery. Years later her bizarre religious beliefs justified her action against my "evil" mother. She had gotten away with it, until Uncle Will began to reexamine the case. . . .

But if she or Aunt Iris had killed Uncle Will, who had put him in the trunk of the car at Tilby's Dream? He wasn't a large man; both women were strong, and either of them could have backed her car up to the car that was burned. Still, how would she get him from the place of the murder into her car and—

A light brush of fingers on my cheek sent me leaping out of my chair.

"I'm sorry," Mr. Gill said. "I didn't mean to startle you. I would never hurt you, dear. You just look so thoughtful and concerned, so much like Joanna."

I remained standing. "Was Mrs. Sanchez angry enough to hurt my mother?"

"What do you mean?"

"Was she angry enough to strike her, to accidentally kill her?"

"Certainly they must have told you. Joanna was killed in a robbery. They never caught the man who did it."

"How do you know it was a man?"

His eyes grew wary. "I simply assumed it."

"Maybe you shouldn't have."

He paled, his face turning the color of skim milk. "This is the result of some peculiar idea of Iris or William. It is natural for you to have questions about what happened, but there is nothing that can be learned so many years after."

"Maybe," I said, edging toward the door. "I'll call you if I have any more questions."

He stood up. "I'll give you a ride home."

"Thanks, but I have a car."

"Did you park out back?" Without giving me a choice, he walked me there.

I couldn't wait to get inside the old Taurus. Mr. Gill leaned down, his face close to the driver's side window. That window worked, but I pretended it didn't.

"Buckle up. Drive safely," he mouthed through the glass.

I turned the key in the ignition and waved.

Hours later, I'd think back to the small parking lot and remember a car with several guys inside, but at that moment, the observation registered as nothing more than relief that other people were around. Believing that I was driving to safety, I took off.

Eighteen

As I DROVE home, I struggled to sort out what I knew. Was there a connection among the deaths of my uncle, my mother, and Mick Sanchez? Three sudden and suspicious deaths created a bewildering number of possibilities. Because the first two occurred fifteen years ago, it seemed impossible to collect the information that would indicate these two deaths were something more than an accident and a robbery. But key bits of information were missing for the recent crime as well.

It wasn't even clear if the use of the abandoned car was evidence of a murderer's plan or a murderer's desperation. Perhaps placing a corpse in a car that was about to be incinerated in a game was a sign of good planning: After all, any evidence indicating where Uncle Will died and how his body was transported to the old Buick would have been driven over by the cars of Erika's friends, and then by the heavy fire trucks. Important clues would have been burned and washed away. On the other hand, if the abandoned car on Tilby's Dream was a location that was easily recognized in a riddle, then it was a location known by most locals. So it could have popped into the head of a murderer who had done no planning at all, a person who had accidentally killed someone and was desperate for a place to dump a body. I was back to square one.

I knew of two people angry enough to get into a fight with Uncle Will: Aunt Iris, fearing he was going to put her away, and Audrey Sanchez, believing he was in league with the devil. Elliot Gill had once been very angry, but why would he hurt Uncle Will after so many years? And then there was Carl, who was obviously worried about the police finding out who was at the fire and who seemed a likely candidate for the earlier harassment of Uncle Will. But even if I came up with solid reasons for these suspects to intentionally or accidentally strike the blow that killed Uncle Will, it wouldn't matter without evidence. The most likely place to find evidence was the site of the murder, which the police didn't seem to know.

But maybe I did. Somehow, before I even arrived in Wisteria, I had seen where the car had burned; some part of me had visited the place. In my second O.B.E., I began somewhere else and ended up at the fire site: What if I was seeing the place where my uncle was struck on the head? Maybe in that O.B.E., I made the journey with him from the time of the attack to the disposal of his body. If I saw the actual place where he was killed, would I recognize it the way I had recognized the fire site?

I pulled into the area at the top of Aunt Iris's driveway, waited for a car to pass, then made a U-turn on Creek Road. Driving to where it forked off Scarborough, I headed away from town toward the large tulip poplar. A storm was brewing. The sky, which had been sullen all afternoon, was growing darker in the west, and when I got to the landmark, its leaves looked pale against the threatening clouds. I turned onto the road that ran through Tilby's Dream and drove between fields of soy and corn. Their vibrant green yellowed in the pre-storm light.

My plan was to check the immediate area, working my way outward from the fire site. I couldn't remember anything at the actual site that looked like a wall with notches in it, but I remembered how Erika's clues, her riddles, were metaphors; maybe the images in my O.B.E.s worked in a similar way. Having turned at the "spring flower" in the riddle, I finally spotted the "green tunnel" and parked my car at its entrance.

I jogged down the dirt road. The old trees and overgrown brush were gloomy, the air oppressive. I was glad to reach the clearing. It was still cordoned off by the yellow police tape. To the left were fields that stretched to the horizon. To the right was a small, uncultivated field hemmed by pine. I walked a ways into the pine trees, perhaps a quarter of a mile, and saw that the wood and its soft floor of needles seemed to go on and on. At that point I stopped. If Uncle Will had been killed here, there would be a limit to how far his body could be easily carried, and the space between the pines was too narrow to drive.

I returned to the burn site, then headed down the road that ran in the opposite direction from which I had come, walking through an identical avenue of trees and passing through open fields. The route curved until I found myself back on what I thought was Scarborough Road, although far enough from the big poplar that I couldn't see it. I turned and retraced my steps.

It occurred to me that, for the murderer, convenience might not have been possible—or even necessary. Given Aunt Iris's habit of coming and going any time of day or night, and her state of confusion, there would be time to kill Uncle Will and move his body before anyone thought to ask where he was or wonder why she hadn't reported him missing.

Since convenience didn't limit the murderer, the crime could have been done anywhere that Uncle Will might go. Obviously, I needed the help of someone familiar with the town and the area around it, someone who would recognize the images in my O.B.E. and guess the riddle they presented.

I wanted to trust Zack, but I couldn't because of his loyalty to Erika. Marcy would be even more familiar with Wisteria and the area around it, but I would have to think of a reason for asking about an image like a notched wall. I could say I had seen the place in one of my mother's photos and I wondered where it was.

When I reached the fire site again, I heard a rumble of thunder. In the open country, it seemed to roll and roll, like a bowling ball thrown down an endless lane. I knew underneath trees were dangerous places to hang out in a storm, but despite what they said on the Weather Channel, I wasn't inclined to seek out a low-lying rut in a field. I crossed the burn site and started through the avenue of trees that led to my car, hoping to beat the storm.

A second peal of thunder sounded closer, and I broke into a jog. The thunder was followed by silence, a long, ominous quiet. A fluttering of birds broke the spell. Wind gusted and branches tossed. I saw a streak of lightning through the trees on the right. I never saw what was coming from the left.

I was hit hard from behind and slammed to the ground. The breath was knocked out of me—I couldn't scream, couldn't fight back. Facedown in the road, I gasped for air. Branches and shells ground into my skin. My mouth got gritty with sand.

I tried to pull my knees up under me, tried to get leverage to stand up, but the person holding me down was heavy. I struggled to cover my head with my arms—all I could think of was Uncle Will struck from behind. But the attacker grabbed my hands and pinned my arms to the ground, bending my wrists at odd angles over the ruts in the road. Now I had my breath again, now I screamed, screamed in pain and fear. I got a knee thrust in my back.

"Listen to me," a male voice said. "Listen, if you don't want to get hurt."

I continued to struggle and got my hair pulled hard. I howled like a beaten puppy.

They laughed. There was more than one.

"Are you listening?"

"Yes," I hissed.

"Stay out of Erika's business."

I strained to pick up my head. "It's my uncle's business I care about."

My face was pushed back in the dirt.

"Stay out of it," said a male voice different from the first. "Your uncle's dead. Don't make us stuff *you* in a trunk."

Their laughter was drowned out by a crack of thunder and a sound like wood splitting. The pressure lightened on me for a second, then I was shoved facedown again. It was raining hard even under the trees, turning the road beneath me into a river of grit. I had to shut my eyes to keep out the splashing sand and mud.

"We're going to let you go, but don't move. We'll be right back on you. Count to a hundred. Do it nice and slow. Don't get up till you've reached the end. Then walk real slow back to your car. Don't tell the police. Don't tell anyone. We'll know. And we won't be so friendly next time."

I was released. As soon as I heard the slap of their racing feet against the road, I lifted my head. I watched the fleeing figures, three of them, until they were erased by rain. I rose shakily to my feet.

I walked slowly, not because they had told me to, but because I was stunned by the attack. I was shocked at how easy it was to overpower me, how quickly I had found myself facedown on the ground and unable to fight back. I walked in a daze, hardly hearing the storm, and finally climbed into my car, soaked to the bone. Lightning flashed over and over; I sat staring up at it dully, as if I were waiting for a traffic light to change. At last I switched on the ignition and headed to the house.

When I pulled into Aunt Iris's driveway, the rain had nearly stopped, but the trees were dripping heavily. My headlights shone like two ghostly beams through the ground mist. I parked and walked toward the front steps. I longed for a shower, not to get rid of the mud, but to clean off the touch of my attackers. I longed for my family.

"Anna."

I jumped a mile.

"Whoa! It's just me."

Zack was standing under the covered porch, backlit by the hall light. I stopped at the foot of the steps, and he started down them. "We need to talk and—my God, what happened to you?"

I backed away from him. When he reached toward me, I put up my hands, instinctively shielding my face. He took my wrists, encircling them with his fingers, holding them gently but firmly. "What happened?"

"I met up with some of your friends."

"Not my friends," he said.

"Okay. Erika's. Three of them."

He turned my hands, examining my scraped palms. "Let's go inside."

"I'll go inside. You go home."

"Did they knock you down?" He crouched to check my knees.

"Obviously."

"Did they do anything else?" His voice sounded as thin and tight as mine.

"Just held me there while they delivered their message."

"Which was?"

"To keep my nose out of Erika's business."

He stood up, took a deep breath, and let it out slowly. "Did they have a weapon?"

"A knee in my back, and my hair—that made a nice weapon; they kept yanking on it, then pushing my face in the road." My voice broke.

"Oh, Anna."

I stiffened and took a step back. Zack was her friend, just like *they* were her friends.

"Where did it happen?"

"Near the fire site. On the dirt road."

"I'll drive you to a doctor."

"I don't need one."

"You should be checked out," he insisted, and took a step closer.

I turned sideways. "I'm just a little rattled."

He laid his hand on my back. As gentle as it was, I winced.

He winced too. "Sorry. I'm sorry. Anna, I am so sorry."

"Go home . . . please. I just need . . . a few minutes by myself." That line had worked the last time.

"Not this time," he said.

I had no energy left to argue. I turned toward the kitchen entrance, and he followed me. The weather and the trees made it seem like twilight. He searched for the wall switch and flicked it on. "Your aunt's car is gone," he observed. "I guess she's out."

"She wanders off at different times. I don't know where."

"Maybe you should put on some dry clothes. I'll help you upstairs."

"No." I lowered myself onto a wooden chair very gingerly.

"Could you have broken any bones?"

"Everything moves. I'm just bruised."

He nodded, then began searching the kitchen cabinets. I watched without asking what he was looking for. I felt as if one huge sob was building in my heart.

Returning with a bowl of water and several soft cloths, he pulled a chair close to mine and began to clean the cuts on my arms. I sat still, watching his hands, the way I used to watch my mother's when I'd had a bad day at dodgeball.

"Did you see the guys who did this to you?"

I shook my head. "Just the backs of them when they were running away. They warned me not to go to the police. They said not to tell anyone. I guess that would include you. They said they would know if I told and they wouldn't be as friendly next time."

I stared at his neck rather than his face and saw him swallow hard. He stood up, brought back fresh water, lukewarm, and gently washed my forehead and cheeks. He knelt on the floor in front of me and examined my knees. "Looks as if you went down on your right one," he said, wetting a clean cloth and touching it lightly to a large brush burn. I stiffened my leg, fighting the instinct to yank it away. He glanced up. "I'm going to pinch your calf. Just a few pinches, okay?"

"I don't think I've ever had a guy goose me on the calf," I replied, trying to joke my way out of the pain.

He did what he said, cleaning the cut and pinching at the same time. "This is how my dad used to do it when I'd come home banged up. The theory is that the pinch sends signals to the brain that help drown out the pain signals from the wound. I thought it was worth a try."

Zack finished cleaning the other leg, then sat back on his heels. "How do you feel?"

"Okay."

"Is there a first-aid kit around, something with an antibiotic ointment?"

"I have a kit in the back of my car. I'll get it later."

"I'll get it for you," he said.

"I'm not helpless." I sounded angry.

There was a moment of tense silence, then he tapped me on the foot. "If there's one thing I'm sure of, it's that *you* are not helpless." He rose and rinsed out the rags, washed out the bowl with soap and water, and laid everything on the drain board.

"Why did you go back to the fire site?" he asked when he was done.

"I was looking for the place where my uncle was murdered."

"The police must have already searched the area," he replied. "The farm is large, with acres of it leased out to other growers, but I'm sure it's been searched thoroughly. When a body is found, everyone starts looking."

"Have you ever seen a place that has a wall with notches along the top, like the wall of a castle? There's a door in the wall or some way to get through. There are pathways and a statue of a rabbit. Have you ever seen anything like that? Outside of Disney World," I added, aware of how silly it sounded.

Zack shook his head no, then looked at me thoughtfully. "But you have. You see things the way a psychic does."

"At night, when I sleep"—I hesitated, but he'd already figured out that something strange was going on inside my head— "I have these things called O.B.E.s, out-of-body experiences."

Zack sat on the kitchen chair next to mine. "You mean like people who are resuscitated? The ones who say they have floated outside their bodies and watched a medical staff working on them?"

"According to the books I've been reading, some people have O.B.E.s even when they're not dying. Last Wednesday night, I thought that I was dreaming about a fire. Kids were there. I heard them laughing and throwing bottles. Then there were sirens and everyone ran. I heard my uncle's voice calling to me, telling me to be careful. A few days later, when I came to Wisteria, I found out he was dead and his body had been burned in a fire that same night. When I went to the site, it was the same place I had seen while sleeping. The night I heard you and Erika talking about me, I was in bed, but somehow, I was there at the fire site, too."

Zack's only response was to blink.

"I've had three O.B.E.s, each time visiting the fire site. But during the last two, I started out in a different place, the one with the wall and the rabbit, and I'm wondering if that is where my uncle started—if somehow I've connected with him and am visiting the place where he was murdered."

"Have you said anything to the sheriff?"

"No. He'd probably think I'm just a crazy O'Neill. I want to try to find the place first. Do you know anything about—"

I was about to mention Audrey's husband when two cats raced past us and hurled themselves against the screen door.

Zack spun around. "What was that?"

"Aunt Iris is coming," I said, getting up to let out the cats.

"How do you know?"

"I don't; the cats do. They line up on Uncle Will's truck and wait for her. I don't want to tell her what has happened—there's no telling how she'll construe it in her head. I'm going to run upstairs and figure out some explanation for my scrapes. You had better go now."

Zack peered through the screen door at the cats. "Unbelievable! It's as if they are waiting for a performance."

"Stay clear of the driveway," I advised. "She stops for nothing but the house."

He reached for the door handle, then turned back. "After Iris gets inside, lock all your doors."

I didn't argue that securing this place was impossible.

"Is your cell phone charged?" he asked.

I nodded.

"Keep it on." He looked around, found a pen, and wrote his number on a paper napkin. "Write down yours."

I did so quickly. I was dangerously close to tears again.

"Anna?" He rested his hands on my shoulders.

I couldn't look at him.

"Anna, you can trust me."

I bit my lip to keep it from trembling.

"You can trust me," he repeated. "But I can see you don't." He turned and left.

I hurried upstairs. The truth was, it was myself I couldn't trust, my eyes from betraying my heart.

Nineteen

I DIDN'T STOP in my room, but headed straight to the bathroom. Ten minutes later, stepping out of a steamy shower, I found ointment and a box of adhesive bandages in the bathroom cabinet. I took care of my cuts, then checked out a row of prescription bottles belonging to Aunt Iris. All of them contained the same prescription and were filled nearly to the top. The dates of all but one were expired; she had missed an awful lot of doses.

I wrapped myself in a towel and peeked out the door. Aunt Iris's door was closed, with a bar of light shining beneath it. Balling up my muddy clothes, I tiptoed down the hall, waiting until I was in Uncle Will's room to call good night to her. As soon as I entered my attic space, I shut the door behind me.

It took a minute to find the knob of the small lamp next to my bed. I turned it on, then took a step back. Stones had been placed on my bed, smooth stones painted with black *X*s or crosses. They were laid in rows, in the same pattern as those placed on Uncle Will's "grave."

Was this a warning—*what happened to William can happen to you*?

I found myself reluctant to touch them. *They're just painted rocks,* I told myself; their power exists only in the mind of the one who attributes it to them: Audrey. What a stupid prank! Having regained my common sense, I reached for a stone on the pillow. She was afraid of me—that's all that this meant. She saw me as another O'Neill, a psychic, a tool of the devil. This was her way of "keeping" me in my place, a safe distance from her.

But if that was her intention, why not put the stones along the gate between the two properties? This arrangement seemed more personal. My bed resembled, a little too closely, a long, narrow grave. How far would Audrey go to make herself safe from the O'Neills? And what was she really afraid of—a family of "evil psychics" or people who might figure out she had killed my mother? Was she the one who had searched the house last night?

I draped my towel over a straight-back chair and pulled on my nightshirt. As ridiculous as it was, I couldn't sleep with the stones nearby. I found a wooden crate, piled them in there, and carried it down to Uncle Will's den. Tomorrow I would confront Audrey with what she had done.

Returning to my bed, I stretched out, physically exhausted but far from sleep. Picking up one of the psychic books, I reread the chapter about induced O.B.E.s, then skipped to the section about how an astral traveler can shape an out-of-body experience, directing himself to certain places. It occurred to me that if I could direct mine, I might be able to pause at the wall, stop next to the rabbit, perhaps even keep myself from "going down the hole" that seemed to take me to the fire. If I could control my journey, and continue to ask to see more clearly, I might discover details that would tell me where that place was.

For the next hour I attempted to induce an O.B.E. My efforts were useless: If there was a psychic part of me, it would not let me control it. The author of the book talked about "letting go," but the more determined and frustrated I became, the harder it was to let go. At last I gave up and turned out my lamp.

I lay back and tried to think about happy things—the games I played with Grace, Claire, and Jack, our senior class trip, Ring Day. . . . My eyes closed. Mental pictures became disjointed, floating by in fragments. My mind had almost shut off.

Suddenly, I sat up. Someone was watching the house.

There hadn't been a sound; I didn't know how I knew—

I just did. I rose quietly and walked to the window nearest my bed. Kneeling there, I scanned the yard. The weather was beginning to clear, but the grass and trees were soaked, their wet surfaces shimmering with moonlight. Clouds dodged the moon, creating liquid shadows.

There! In the shadow of the big tree something moved. I waited, barely breathing. The edge of the shadow separated from the tree's darkness and became the figure of a man: Elliot Gill.

He gazed up at the house. He was too far away for me to see the expression on his face, but his head was raised, the angle of his body attentive, like that of a worshipper at a shrine—or a hunter sighting his target. My skin crept. Was he obsessed and pitiful, or obsessed and dangerous?

He started walking toward the house. *I should have listened to Zack,* I thought; at least I could have made it harder for someone to get in. If I started locking up now, Mr. Gill was sure to hear me. Did I want him to know that I saw him? If I turned on a light, would it deter him or draw him to me?

I wondered how long it would take the sheriff to respond to a call. Then I remembered: My cell phone was charged, but it was in my purse, in my car. Aunt Iris's landline was in the downstairs hall.

Keeping the lights off, I hurried through Uncle Will's room

to the hall. I didn't know how Aunt Iris would react and decided that I'd wake her only as a last resort. I crept down the stairs. The front door was closed, and I quietly turned the latch to lock it. The back door of the hall was open, a rectangle of moonlight shining on the floor, nothing but an unlocked screen between me and Mr. Gill.

I found the phone and lifted the receiver. It was old and did not have a lighted pad; I felt the keys, reminding myself where the numbers 9 and 1 were—bottom right and top left corners.

I was reluctant to call the police. Aunt Iris was just paranoid enough to imagine that they had come to carry her off to "the crazy-people place." I could call Zack. His cell phone number was . . . upstairs in the pocket of my muddy pants.

The dial tone changed to a ring, then a recorded voice, "If you would like to make a call, please hang up and—"

In the silence of the house, the voice sounded loud. I quickly put the receiver down and looked toward the screen door. My heart stopped. Elliot Gill was standing ten feet from the house, looking up at the second-floor windows, unaware of me watching him from the floor below. I pressed 9. My finger hovered over the 1.

Then he turned abruptly, looking to the right. Something had caught his eye, movement on the other side of the yard. He craned his neck, as if trying to get a better look, then took off, moving parallel to the house, as if he intended to run around it.

I dropped the phone and raced to the back door to close and lock it. Someone else passed by, moving fast. I couldn't see who. I hurried to the living room, but the bushes blocked my view, both at the side and front windows. I crossed the hall to the dining room. Knowing the kitchen door was probably open, I looked out the window before going any farther.

Zack. Stopping by the cars, he turned on a large flashlight, shining its beam up the driveway.

He must have followed Mr. Gill around the house. If Mr. Gill, realizing someone was watching him, had fled the property, his only choices were the path to the Flemings' house or the driveway; the scrubby bank up to the bridge would be difficult to climb, especially in the dark.

After a minute of watching, Zack directed the beam at his feet, where a cat rubbed his legs. He sat down next to the cat, sharing his blanket with it. In the halo cast by the flashlight, I saw a stuffed knapsack and the gleam of a long, cylindrical object—a thermos. Zack was keeping watch over me.

Tears ran down my face before I could stop them. I went upstairs, lay down in bed, and, feeling safe, fell sound asleep.

When I awoke Saturday morning, Zack was gone. Before going downstairs, I took aspirin and tried to work the stiffness out of my body with stretching exercises. Glad that Marcy kept her shop so cool, I put on a long-sleeved shirt and pants and left my hair loose so it would swing forward and make less noticeable the scrapes on my face.

Aunt Iris was already in the kitchen, wearing one of her billowy dresses and a pair of flip-flops. "G'morning."

"I prefer your hair up," she responded. Having poured dry cereal into a coffee mug, she was "drinking" it.

"Aunt Iris, when I got home last night, I found some stones on my bed."

She chewed and said nothing.

"They were painted like the ones Audrey placed over the hole where you buried Uncle Will's ashes. I put the stones in a box and left them in the den. When you've finished your cereal, will you come see?"

"I know what they look like."

"They were arranged on my bed," I went on, "in the same pattern as those placed on the ashes."

Aunt Iris raised her mug of Cheerios to her mouth and gazed at me above the rim.

"Do you know why?" I asked.

"No."

"Well, can you guess why?"

"I don't wish to."

I turned on the teakettle, then tried another tactic. "What do stones that are painted like that mean?"

"Whatever you want them to mean."

"I don't *want* them to mean anything."

"Then why did you ask?"

She tipped the mug and made small mouse noises, crunching on her cereal. I felt like banging my head against the kitchen cabinets.

I carried my tea to Uncle Will's den and sat for a few minutes, studying the stones that had been laid on my bed. They were obviously hand-painted. I carried two of them outside to compare them to the ones that had been set on Uncle Will's plot—they were very similar—then headed toward the Flemings' house, hoping Audrey would answer the door.

When I reached the gate between the two properties, I saw Clyde racing toward the creek in an effort to catch up with his duck friends. Audrey stood on the patio, watching him, her arms crossed.

"Mrs. Sanchez," I called. "Mrs. Sanchez!"

She cocked her head and looked about.

"Can I talk to you?"

"Yes. Yes, I'm coming." She walked briskly toward me, meeting me halfway between the gate and the house.

I held out the rocks. "I found these on my bed last night."

She stared down at them. "You found these—on your bed, you say?"

"They're like the ones you placed on Uncle Will's plot of ashes."

She frowned.

"I saw you the night you put them there."

She glanced up at me, her brow knitted with concern.

"Why did you put these on my bed, Mrs. Sanchez?"

Audrey's tiny upper teeth pressed into her lower lip. "Iris must have."

"But I saw you do it! I saw you put them on my uncle's plot."

"I mean Iris must have put them on your bed. She's imitating me—I don't know why." Audrey looked toward the house and shook her head. "You must be very careful, child," she said, moving away from the stones, as if she thought it unwise to stand too close to them. "Don't let what happened to me happen to you."

"Meaning?"

"I was lured into believing in them, in their special powers. They will betray you."

"They . . . who?"

"You know who I mean."

"But I don't," I insisted. "Are you referring to my mother?

My great-aunt? I know that you were a client of my mother. You depended on her, then you blamed her when your husband died. You thought she should have foreseen the accident and warned you."

Audrey's lips pulled over her tiny teeth. "Psychics are the tools of the devil. Joanna tempted me with knowledge not meant for human minds, and I was punished. So was William, but his debt is paid now. Better fire here than fire hereafter."

"The fire *here* was set by kids, people who didn't know he was in the car."

"Willing or unwilling," she replied, "knowing or not, any one of us might be called to do God's work. Joanna's killer saved her soul, ending her life before she could delve too far into evil."

I stared at the woman in disbelief. "You're saying her soul was saved by a thief and murderer?"

"Sometimes the least among us are chosen for holy work."

I shook my head. People who attributed events that *they* desired to God's will were crazy—and dangerous.

Audrey reached for me. Her fingers felt dry and papery on my arm. "You look upset, child. You see what Iris is trying to do, don't you? She is telling you these things to turn you against me. She fears I will convert you."

"It was Elliot Gill who told me."

"Elliot." She said the name with distaste. "Do not trust

him. He was obsessed with your mother, and obsession does not come from God."

"How about forgiveness?" I asked. "Where does that come from?"

"I will give Elliot a little credit," Audrey said. "He contacted Social Services and told them what was going on in that house and that a child's life was in danger."

"Meaning me."

"After your mother died, he called Social Services, and you were finally moved out of there. William hated him for it. It is true that Elliot's reason for doing that was revenge—he was still angry at William for discouraging Joanna's affections. But all's well that ends well. You were out of that house of evil. You see now why I feel I must help you leave again, before you come under her influence."

I saw now a lot of things: the intense dislike between my uncle and Elliot Gill; the extreme views of Audrey that would allow her to sanction even acts of violence; and the long-term mental problems of my great-aunt. What I couldn't see was which of these things had led to the death of my uncle.

Twenty

AFTER LEAVING AUDREY, I considered dumping the stones in the creek, but I changed my mind and left the crate in Uncle Will's den. As soon as I had time, I would get a magnifying glass and compare the two sets more carefully to see if there were telltale differences, enough to suggest that Audrey was telling the truth. When I passed through the kitchen, Aunt Iris was gone, her mug of cereal left behind. I ate a quick breakfast and headed for work.

Marcy greeted me with a preoccupied hello, followed a moment later by a quick survey of my outfit. "Am I keeping the temperature too cool for you?"

I faked a laugh. "No, I haven't had a chance to do laundry. These are my only clean clothes."

It was a lame excuse, but I thought she believed it. Fifteen minutes later, when we were ready for business, she leaned over the glass counter where I was standing and pushed back my hair, revealing the long scrape on my cheek. "How did it happen?" she asked. When I didn't respond immediately, she added, "What are you hiding beneath your long sleeves?"

"Just a few bruises."

"How did it happen?" Marcy repeated.

"I fell. Tripped, actually. Aunt Iris doesn't like to keep lights on. The house is really dark at night."

"How many times did you fall?"

I hesitated, and she didn't wait for me to fumble into a lie. "There are scrapes on both sides of your face, widely spaced scrapes, close to each ear."

Which meant, of course, I had to fall at least once on each side—kind of clumsy, even for me.

"I want a straight answer, Anna. What happened?"

"I ran into some kids who don't like me."

Marcy tilted her head to one side, her light eyes studying me. "You're not a girl inclined to get into that sort of trouble. You're too smart."

"You would think so."

"What are you afraid to tell me?" she asked. "Were you molested?"

"No," I replied quickly. "Just knocked down."

"By whom?"

"I don't know. They pushed me down face-first. I saw their

backs when they were running away, but it was raining hard. It was during yesterday's storm."

"Where?"

"Tilby's Dream."

She frowned. "You went back there again—to the place of the fire? Why?"

"I just wanted to."

She studied my face, then shook her head, as if I didn't get it. "Anna, this may seem like a small, innocent-looking town, but we have some kids here who are spoiled rotten and bored. They're out of control. They consider burning someone else's property a party game."

"I know."

"You should have come over last night. You should have come to my house."

"When I got home, Zack was waiting on the porch for me. I told him what happened, and he helped me get cleaned up."

"Then *he* should have told me," she said, sounding frustrated. "He should have brought you to our house. You called the sheriff, I assume."

"Not yet."

"All right," she said brusquely, "I will." She reached under the counter and pulled out her cell phone.

"No, don't! Please don't."

"Why not?"

"For one thing, I was told that if I did, there are others who'll come after me."

"That line is older than Hollywood," Marcy responded, and flicked open her phone.

"For another, it could mess up my effort to figure out what happened to Uncle Will."

Her blue eyes held mine for a moment, her gaze long and thoughtful.

"The guys are friends of the person who set the fire. The arsonist communicates by texting. It's important for me to find out who is on the contacts list. I think that one of the kids, or someone else who has access to their messages, used the arson as a cover-up for my uncle's murder. I don't want to stir up these guys, not yet. I don't want them putting pressure on other kids to keep quiet. I need to research a few more things before I go to the police."

"Anna, you're in over your head."

"Give me till Monday morning. I'll go to the sheriff then. Promise!"

She sighed, then closed the phone. "If you don't make the call on Monday, I will."

"Deal," I said, hoping to argue her out of it on Monday, and if that didn't work, to convince the sheriff I'd be more help to him if he didn't take immediate action.

Five minutes later our first customer came in. Last night's storm had cooled down the weather, and business remained steady through lunchtime. After lunch a tour bus passed through. The jingling of the door's sleigh bells didn't stop till Marcy flipped over the CLOSED sign. "I could use a few more days like this," she said.

"Me too. I like it busy."

She collected our purses from the locked cabinet. "Did Zack give you the number for our house?"

"Just his cell."

She printed neatly on a piece of paper. "Here's the landline. You already have my cell number. Try that first. If you have any concerns about your own safety—or about Iris—call me."

"Thanks."

She set the store alarm and turned out the lights.

"How is Iris doing?" she asked as we walked to our cars.

"Not so good. She gets the present and past mixed up, and I think I'm making it worse."

"I'm sure your presence has stirred up a lot of memories."

"She argues with Uncle Will as if she sees him, and some of those arguments are about whether or not to keep a child."

Marcy squinted at me in the slanting sun. "Meaning you. She must be reliving arguments that occurred after your mother died."

"Sometimes she talks to me as if *I'm* Joanna, which may not be so crazy—I look a lot like my birth mother. I wish I knew how to help her."

"I know you are concerned about her, Anna, but right now you must look out for yourself. This research you are doing before talking to the sheriff, what does it involve?"

"Just reading old newspapers," I replied.

Marcy opened her car door. "All right, then. See you soon." She turned to look at me. "Promise to call me if a problem arises, day or night, no matter the time."

"Sure," I said.

"Sure," she repeated with a wry smile, as if she guessed I wouldn't.

I planned to ask Marcy about Audrey and Mick Sanchez, but not until I knew a little more. Loyalty was important to Marcy, and she might sugarcoat her answers to cover for the person who had always taken care of her. I hoped the newspaper that reported Joanna's death had also reported Mick's accident.

Both the public and college libraries were closed on Saturday evening, but it was possible that the paper's archives were online. Parking my car at the top of High Street, I walked to the only real hotel in town, looking for Internet access. I got lucky with a café at the rear of the hotel, but unlucky with the website that belonged to the paper: Its archives ran back only a year and a half. There was one phone number and two e-mail addresses: editor@ and adverts@. I typed to the first:

WHEN R U OPEN?

I was messaged right back. FOR AS LONG AS I'M HERE.

WOULD LIKE 2 COME BY. I thought for a moment, then typed the only bait I could think of: STOPPING @ TEA LEAVES. WANT SOMETHING?

I DOUB ESPR + I REG COFFEE MED SZ W/2 CREAMS & 4 DNUTS. I'M UPSTAIRS.

Fifteen minutes later I stood on Heron Street in front of a shingled storefront with stairs running up the outside of the building. I climbed the wooden steps and knocked on the door.

"It's open."

With one hand balancing my tray of drinks, the other grasping the bag of doughnuts and door handle, I pushed door open with my foot.

The man inside hopped up. "Oh, sorry," he said, taking the tray and bag from me and setting them on a table. He held out his hand. "Tom Wittstadt. Editor in chief, editor in minor, editor ed-cetera."

He was medium height with a full face, curly salt-and-pepper hair, and a bit of a belly under his blue Hawaiian shirt.

"And this is Hero." A black Lab, lying close to the chair where Wittstadt had been sitting, thumped his tail.

"Hello, Hero."

The dog lifted his head, his nose quivering. His eyes were opaque.

"He can't see you, so he sniffs a lot," the editor explained. "Usually he stays put. You okay with dogs?"

"Yeah, sure. Can I pet him?"

The editor nodded. "Just talk to him and let him know you're coming."

"How're you doing, Hero?" I said, moving toward him slowly. "Are you the brains behind this paper?" Silently I asked, *Do you like to be petted, or do you just put up with it?*

Hero pulled himself to his feet and walked toward me.

"Whoa! You must smell good," Mr. Wittstadt said.

Hey, buddy.

The dog nosed my face gently, then licked me in the crease of my neck.

You like salt, huh? Where do you like to be petted? Those little dimples behind your ears? I scratched them.

"Are you by any chance related to Iris O'Neill?" the editor asked.

I sighed. "My hair?"

"No, the way you are with Hero. He likes Iris, too."

I smiled. "I'm her great-niece, Anna. Anna O'Neill Kirkpatrick."

"Nice to meet you, Anna. I'm sorry about William."

The editor pulled out his wallet, then dug in his jeans for change. The office was littered with paper—piles of it, balls of it, odd-shaped scraps of it. A worktable occupied the center of the room, with ancient office furniture filling up the rest of the space. The gray walls were decorated with maps and several posters of old music icons; I recognized Bob Dylan. On a shelf above Wittstadt's desk was a row of bobbleheads, most of them Ravens and Orioles.

"How's Iris doing?"

"Okay." I stood up and retrieved the iced tea that I had bought myself. The editor handed me the exact amount for his order.

"You know, I tried to interview her," he said. "She went psychic on me."

"Psychic or psycho?" I asked.

I watched him empty out a tall travel mug, giving a drink to a plant, then pour both the double espresso and the regular coffee into the mug. "Psych*ic*. That wily old woman, I think she was faking it. Mind you, I'm not saying she's a fake. I just think she was pretending at the moment, because she didn't want to answer my questions."

"Could be."

"Has Iris told you what she thinks happened to William?"

"No."

He sipped. "Got any ideas of your own?"

"No."

"Doughnut?" he offered.

"No thanks."

He pulled off a piece with his teeth. "Have you been in touch with McManus?"

"A few days ago, just to find out what the police know so far."

"Which is?"

"Probably the same thing he told you."

Wittstadt smiled. "So why are you here, other than to torture a newspaper guy with short answers, all of which he already knew?"

"I'd like to look in your archives."

"Yeah?"

"I went online. They go back only a year and a half."

He laughed. "Because I go back only a year and a half. That's when I bought this prestigious paper." He led the way to a rear room. I followed him to stacks that were illuminated by old fluorescent-tube lights, the shelves labeled in a hand-scrawl that was yellowed over with tape.

"What date do you want?"

I told him the year. "I guess you don't have an index."

Wittstadt snorted. "Is there a particular thing you are looking for so we can narrow the possibilities? You know, like a fishing report?"

Despite his easygoing manner, he'd be checking the archives later to see what I was researching. He'd guess it was connected to the O'Neills. But if he was relatively new to Wisteria, he wouldn't know anything about Mick Sanchez.

"An obituary."

I saw the light flicker in his eyes. "Well, that's easy. They are always on the second-to-last page. Always," he repeated. "I've tried to redesign the paper, but each time I do, my advertisers throw a fit. I'm just lucky the old publisher stopped using 'thee' and 'thou' before I took over."

I smiled.

"I'll leave you to your search, Anna. Careful with the drink, okay?"

"Sure."

Since the paper was a weekly and I knew the end date would be mid-August, a week after Joanna's death, my first search wouldn't take long. I found the article on her, the one Uncle Will had enclosed with his letter, and reread it. There was a copy machine in the office, but I figured that asking to use it would invite more questions from Mr. Wittstadt. When

I retrieved a sheet of paper from a recycle bin and picked up a pencil on the worktable, he watched me but didn't comment. I jotted down details, then worked my way backward through the weeks of July, June, and May.

In the May 8 edition I discovered a short death notice announcing Mick Sanchez's services and burial. I turned to the first page and combed through the newspaper, but there was no mention of the accident. Figuring that the death had come as a surprise and Audrey may have needed extra time to make funeral arrangements, I searched the previous edition. On page 3, I found it.

FATAL ACCIDENT ON SCARBOROUGH RD.
On the rainy evening of April 27, at approximately 7:00 p.m., Miguel Sanchez lost control of his vehicle on Scarborough Road about 4.5 miles past Wist Creek Bridge. He was pronounced dead at the scene.

The victim, on prescription medication for a heart condition for the last two years, suffered a cardiac arrest. Police believe the medical emergency precipitated the accident.

Sanchez, known as "Mick," came from Chincoteague, Virginia, and had been the gardener for the Fairfax family of Oyster Creek for the last 26 years. He and his wife, Audrey (nee Randolph), also a Fairfax employee, were married for 23 years and lived at the Oyster Creek estate. They had no children. His wife is his sole survivor.

After rereading it several times, I wondered why Audrey or Joanna would have been surprised by his death. People dropped dead from heart attacks without any kind of warning, and the man was known to have a heart condition. This information was useless, just more evidence that Audrey got obsessive. Still, I copied down the essentials:

> *April 27, 7 p.m., 4.5 miles / WC Bridge*
>
> *Chincoteague, VA. 23 yrs – Audrey Randolph*
>
> *26 yrs – Fairfax garden – heart condition*

Perhaps it was the way I arranged the words on the page, or perhaps there was a similarity between my mother's handwriting and my own, but my eyes, focusing on "garden" and "heart," suddenly saw those words on a different page. In my mother's poem there was a garden shaped like a heart. I remembered that a snake wrapped itself around a heart of flowers, making the flowers wilt. It was a haunting image, a picture of a heart being constricted and killed—a kind of heart attack. Could the poem be about Mick's death?

Mr. Gill had said that my mother's failure to foresee Mick's accident and warn Audrey had upset her. People write about things that really upset them. And she had placed the poem in her client book.

I quickly returned the stack of newspapers to the shelf, snatched up my tea, and said a hasty good-bye to Mr. Wittstadt and Hero. I ran all the way to my car, impatient to get home and read my mother's poem. When a psychic wrote poetry, what kind of truths were locked inside her images?

Twenty-one

AUNT IRIS'S GOLD sedan was parked in its usual spot. Climbing out of my car, I scanned the windows of the house, wondering which room she was in. The army of cats greeted me, some mewing and rubbing against my legs as if they wanted to be fed, but when I approached the kitchen door, they backed off and slinked away.

Entering the kitchen, I paused to listen for movement in the house. It was silent. I tiptoed to Aunt Iris's office, eased the door open, and found the room empty. I was tempted to go straight to Uncle Will's den and retrieve the notebook. Then a loud crash made me spin around. I ran toward the noise, through the dining room to the center hall. Aunt Iris stood in front of a mirror that hung above the phone table. Her face quivering with fury, she slammed a hammer against the glass again and again.

"Aunt Iris!"

With her bare fingers, she pulled at a shard of silver that remained in the corner of the frame, trying to free it. I saw a trickle of blood. She didn't flinch.

"Aunt Iris, stop!"

She swung the hammer at the frame's backing, though only the corner sliver was left.

"Stop!"

A large fragment of the mirror lay on the table. Seeing it, she raised her hammer and brought it down swiftly. Shards exploded, jagged pieces of glass flying everywhere.

I stepped back into the dining room. Part of me wanted to run; the other part was afraid to leave my aunt alone. I picked up a candlestick—as if a sane person clutching a candlestick would be a match against an insane one wielding a hammer! Entering the hall again, I found her banging a small piece of glass on the corner of the table, hammering it until the fragments were glitter.

"Stop it!" I screamed at her. "Stop it now!"

She froze. Her eyes traveled up my right arm, and she shrank from me. "Put it down," she said, staring at the candlestick.

"After you put down your hammer," I replied.

She licked her lips. She began to whimper: "Don't do it. Please don't do it." She dropped the hammer and ran upstairs.

I set down the candlestick, surprised, and then I remembered: When my mother was killed, two candlesticks were missing, and they never found the murder weapon. My hands shook. I had to sit on the steps for a few minutes. Finally, I rose to sweep the hall. When the glass was cleaned up, I climbed the stairs to check on my aunt.

She had left her door open and lay motionless on her bed. With the press of trees outside her window and the shades pulled, it was nearly night in her room. I tiptoed toward her.

"Who's there?"

I took a half step back. "Anna. Just Anna. How are you feeling, Aunt Iris?"

She didn't reply. Her hands were folded and resting on her stomach. A loosely rolled towel covered her eyes.

"Do you have a headache?" I asked.

Still, she didn't answer.

"What can I do to help?"

"Make them stop," she said. "Make them stop talking."

"They—who?"

"They're talking their fool heads off."

"You mean the voices?"

"They won't leave me alone."

I moved closer. "What are they saying?"

She didn't reply.

"Aunt Iris, what are the voices saying?"

"I can't tell you."

She lay as still as death.

"Why did you break the mirror?" I asked.

"They were making faces at me."

"You mean the voices—they have faces?"

She shuddered. "Every time I looked in the mirror, some-one was making a dreadful face at me."

What face could she have seen except her own? I thought. But perhaps a mirror was like a psychic's glass, a crystal ball. Perhaps she could see ghosts of the past in it.

"Did you see someone—in the mirror—who doesn't like you?"

She didn't reply.

"Maybe you saw Uncle Will. Were you and Uncle Will arguing again?"

She remained silent. I felt as if all the answers I wanted were locked inside her head, and I couldn't find the question to open the vault.

"I'm tired," she said. "I want to be alone."

"All right. Get some rest. I'll be downstairs."

I checked the other rooms for broken objects, then returned to the first floor and checked the living room. Given the num-ber of candlesticks, heavy lamps, and knives in the house, I felt silly locking the hammer in the trunk of my car, but I would have felt even sillier if I had left it out and she used it again. Then I headed for the den, hoping that Aunt Iris would sleep for a while and give me time to study my mother's notebook.

I found it where I had left it, behind a row of books, and carefully unfolded the old newspaper it was wrapped in. The journal's entries started in January of the year my mother died. While other clients were listed only once a week or once a month, appointments for the initials A.S. appeared twice a week or more. About half of the entries, which I assumed were for Audrey Sanchez, had been marked "Paid."

I found an appointment for A.S. two days before Mick Sanchez's accident. An appointment that had been set for the day after the accident was scratched out. Another appointment, four days after, was also crossed out. The final listing I found for A.S. was exactly one week after Mick Sanchez's death. It was checked off, as were other appointments that Audrey appeared to have kept. I wondered if there had been a big blowup that day.

At some point I needed to examine the book line by line, but I was impatient to get to the poem. I carried them both to Uncle Will's desk, sat down, and unfolded the paper to read.

The seed cracks open, the green sprout
of a plant emerges—

a green snake.
The snake slides past a rabbit,
glides past a cat.
Winding itself around flowers—
a garden shaped like a heart—
the snake turns to me.
It wears a mask.
Flowers wilt.

I had remembered correctly the second half of the poem. The sentence structure was inverted, but "snake" was the subject—it was the snake winding itself around flowers, winding itself around a garden shaped like a heart. I imagined a heart of flowers, something like a picture on a Valentine's Day card, being wrapped and squeezed by a snake till all the flowers wilted. But what was this "mask" thing all about? Perhaps the snake was in disguise—or rather, the snake itself was some kind of disguise. This much I understood: Whatever was killing the heart of flowers, it was *not* what it appeared to be.

I backed up in the poem. The snake had come out of a seed. I imagined it looking like a green sprout from a germinating seed, but growing into a snake. So . . . so what appeared to be good was really bad. What appeared to be as harmless as an emerging flower was really an evil snake.

I moved on to the other animals. Why had my mother bothered to include them? I stared at them, puzzled, then tried to think about the images the way an English teacher would. A rabbit was a symbol of fertility, as in the phrase "breeding like rabbits." It was a symbol of spring, as in the Easter Bunny. Rabbits were shy, gentle, innocent-looking creatures. Cats, on the other hand, were connected with witches and often perceived as sneaky predators in the natural world. Symbolically, they were not innocent. So what did this mean? A rabbit and a cat—innocence and sneakiness, prey and predator—

"What are you reading?"

I jumped at the sound of Aunt Iris's voice. She was standing a few feet from me on the other side of the desk, having entered the room as quietly as a cat.

"Joanna, what are you doing?"

So I was my mother again. "Checking through my appointment book," I replied.

She stepped closer to the desk, eyed the notebook, then picked up the sheet of paper resting on it. "What is this?"

"A poem."

She read it, her face tense with concentration. Then her eyes lifted slowly above the edge of the paper, locking on mine. "You're working," she said accusingly. "This is a reading."

A reading—as in *psychic reading*, I thought. Maybe when a psychic saw images—in a crystal ball or anywhere else—they weren't necessarily literal images. They weren't photographic glimpses, but symbols, like symbols on Tarot cards, like symbols in a poem. She had to interpret what she was seeing, had to read into them the way you read into a poem. Which is what my mother was doing, jotting down and mulling over images she had accessed psychically, trying to understand Mick's death and how she had missed foreseeing it.

"That's right," I said, taking the paper from my aunt, laying it down on the book again. "I was thinking about Mick Sanchez."

"But it was an accident. An accident!" she insisted, then snatched the paper and book, and ran out of the room.

I had seen the look in her eyes: one of fear. Not surprise, not anger. *Fear.* Of what? What didn't she want me—Joanna—to figure out through a psychic reading?

Her footsteps along the porch ended with the slam of a screen door. She was in the kitchen. I suddenly realized what she could do and raced after her. Entering the kitchen, I saw the stove's blue flames leap up to the sheet of paper. It curled into a black leaf. She turned another knob on the stove, and I saw that the notebook was on the back burner. I rushed forward. Shoving her aside, I turned the greasy knob, but the book had already caught fire. I picked it up by the corner and threw it into the sink. Turning on the faucet, I let the cold water run over the book and my arm. The underside of my wrist felt burned. What was left of my mother's book hissed into a crumpled mess.

"Why did you do this?" I cried.

"I told you before, Joanna, it's dangerous to pry into the secrets of others."

"What secrets?" I demanded.

"I warned you. Only animals can be trusted. People will turn on you."

"People like Audrey?"

She put her hands over her eyes, as if she were trying to block out what she saw. "Forget about Mick. It was an accident."

Her fear and insistence made me think his death was anything but.

I remembered her first mention of Mick and how puzzled she was when I, trying to play the role of my mother, had referred to him as "my lover." I remembered the tone of surprise: "*Your* lover?" Of course, Mick was a generation too old for my mother. He was Audrey's age; he was Iris's age. What if he had been Aunt Iris's boyfriend? Was this one of the secrets that she could never tell?

If I asked directly, she would probably deny it. I had to cast the question in another form. "Aunt Iris, why did Mick choose to marry Audrey?"

She stood still, her fingers gripping the knobs of the stove, and for a moment I thought she was going to turn it back on. I set my hands lightly on her arms. "Why didn't he marry you?"

She pulled away from me. The large frame of her body bent forward and her shoulders sagged. I began to regret my question.

At last she spoke, her voice rough. "He said I was crazy. He said I was sick. He said I was too sick in the head to raise a child. That's what he said."

"I'm sorry."

"He was afraid of me."

"I'm really sorry." I lay my hand on her back, but she slipped away, withdrawing into the dining room, walking slowly down the hall, climbing the steps quietly.

I didn't like Mick Sanchez. If I discovered that my great-aunt had killed him, I wasn't sure I would tell the police. But I had to know, because it looked as if Joanna had been trying to find out the same thing and had paid the price for it.

Picking up a pen, I jotted on a napkin the images and wording I could remember from the poem. As I wrote, I became aware of the stinging heat in my wrist. I got up to retrieve some ice from the freezer.

It had become a habit, reaching up to catch the large,

speckled fish before it fell on my foot. But there was no fish today. I looked in the shelves and bins of the lower part of the fridge, then in the trash can. I'd have smelled the fish if Aunt Iris had cooked it. I looked out the back of the house. Maybe she threw it into the creek. Maybe she thought it would perk up and swim away.

Returning to the kitchen, I wrapped a chunk of ice in a dish towel and held the cold pack against my wrist, studying the images I had written down.

Did the snake represent a sneaky form of killing—something that masked itself as a naturally occurring heart attack? Were the rabbit and cat symbolic of other people who had been involved? The turbulent emotions of the last week and lack of sleep were catching up with me: Images shifted in my mind like the colored shapes in a kaleidoscope. I needed fresh air to clear my head. I went upstairs to change into shorts and running shoes. After checking on Aunt Iris, finding her asleep in her room, I grabbed an apple and headed out for a walk.

The gardens once kept by Mick Sanchez were a short distance away. What if there was a literal basis for my mother's images, something concrete and specific that tied her garden symbols to Mick? Perhaps if I saw the gardens, the images would make more sense. With less than an hour of sunlight left, I hurried to the Fairfax estate.

Twenty-two

FIFTY MINUTES LATER I stood scowling at the Fairfaxes' fence, tall metal bars that ended in an earthy-smelling marsh. The ground had turned soft and wet beneath my feet, and with each step, I sank in deeper, my footprints becoming puddles. The high river grass was alive with whining insects. I imagined that snakes liked it too.

I hadn't been able to enter the property from the road. The estate's large gates had been locked electrically. There was a keypad for punching in codes, and I had tried some obvious ones without luck. If there was a caretaker on the property, he hadn't responded to the intercom button that I'd pressed repeatedly. So I'd followed the iron fence, thinking there might be a service or employee entrance, and discovered a smaller gate with a narrow driveway. But it, too, was locked electrically and didn't accept the random codes that I'd tried. I'd peered through the bars; if there was a car parked inside, the landscaping prevented me from seeing it. The left side of the property was thick with trees, so I'd turned back and searched on the right side instead, moving toward the Flemings' property. There was no break in the fence, not until it ended where I was standing now, in a marsh.

I did not want to wade any farther into the muck, not in the growing darkness. I realized that Marcy might know the gate codes, but she'd ask questions I didn't want to answer yet. And this time, I knew, there would be an immediate call to the sheriff. I would have to be patient and search again in daylight.

I took a shortcut across the Flemings' property. No one was on the terrace. Ducks waddled fearlessly on the lower lawn. Beneath the dock light, the cabin cruiser and rowboat rocked gently. The rowboat!

I tried to recall the water approach to the Fairfax property. The house sat on top of a hill, with all but its roof invisible behind the trees. The shoreline itself was crescent-shaped, the creek cutting into the land. As I remembered it, the drop from lawn to water was a steep clay and sand bank, a wall of erosion high enough to make climbing difficult. With the family gone, there was no place for docking and no wooden steps up to the lawn. But if the rowboat could be nosed onto the tiny strip of beach, I might be able to climb up—especially if Zack gave me a hand.

I walked quickly around the Flemings' house to the front. I heard Clyde baying before I reached the porch. He stopped, as if silenced. As soon as I rang the bell, Audrey answered the door.

"She's gone off, hasn't she! I knew she would. These things work in cycles."

"No, Aunt Iris is fine," I replied. "May I speak with Zack, please?"

"He isn't home. I knew it was going to be a bad night," Audrey went on, her eyes peering into the darkness behind me as if she saw signs of evil hanging from the trees. "When I took the dog out, I heard Iris screaming like a banshee."

I was curious now. "What was she saying?"

"It was gibberish, all gibberish. The devil's language."

"I see. Do you know when Zack will be home?"

Audrey shook her head. "He went out with that girl."

"Erika?"

She nodded.

"May I leave a note for Zack?" I had his cell phone number, but I wasn't going to call him, not when he was with Erika.

"Of course. Come in. We'll talk."

"Thanks, but I just want to leave a note for Zack."

I saw the change in her eyes. Lips pursed in disapproval, she let me in and begrudgingly provided pen and paper, watching my hand as I wrote. I figured that even if my note were folded and taped, Audrey would read it, so I left out details, simply asking Zack to call me no matter how late he got in.

"Please make sure he gets this tonight," I said, handing the note to her.

When I returned to the house, I found several of the cats lounging around the kitchen and a few nuggets of fresh food scattered around an empty platter on the floor. Aunt Iris must have gotten up and fed them. I checked out front and saw that her car was gone.

For a moment I considered calling the sheriff, but what could I say—that I was worried because Aunt Iris had smashed a mirror, laid down for a nap, and then gone out? When I left her, the violent behavior appeared to be over. And it was, after all, nine o'clock on a Saturday night, a time when a lot of people went out. Besides, she had left the house at stranger times than this.

Of course, McManus would come if I told him I had some ideas about Uncle Will's death, but all I really had was a pile of disjointed theories. I paced for an hour, waiting for something to happen: Zack to call, Aunt Iris to return, the images from my mother's notebook to fall into a pattern that I understood. Finally, I couldn't stand it any longer.

I searched the house for a stepladder, found a three-foot

one, and carried it with a flashlight to the Flemings' dock. The moon, which had glowed yellow at its rising, shone whiter and more brightly now. For the next fifteen minutes I focused on the task of launching the boat and rowing it through the dark. It was hard to judge distance without being able to see the shoreline. I felt as if I had rowed miles when I finally caught the glint of moonlight on the rooftop and chimneys of the Fairfax house. I turned toward shore. As I rowed closer to the sandy bank, I pushed one of the oars straight down in the water to gauge the depth. I couldn't touch bottom. I got goose bumps all over—I really don't like dark water. But I continued to test every ten feet or so, afraid that if I ran the boat aground, I'd damage it.

When the depth dropped to two feet, I gingerly climbed into the dark creek. My wet shoes felt heavy on my feet and kept slipping on the river stones. The boat had an anchor, but I didn't know how to make sure it would catch and hold in the creek bottom. I towed the boat a short distance, then carried the anchor to shore. I dug a hole, dropped in the anchor, and pushed the heavy sand over it.

By the time I had done that, the long line for the anchor had unreeled and the boat had floated away from shore. I waded out again, hating the way the currents swirled and eddied around my legs, imagining eels and other slimy things. I towed the boat a second time and shortened its rope with a knot. Then I carried the flashlight and ladder to shore and set the ladder close to the bank. Climbing to its top, I found the edge of the lawn was even with my shoulders.

I tried to pull myself up and over the edge, grabbing handfuls of grass. Tufts tore off, spraying sand in my face. I tried again and created a small landslide. Looking to either side of me, I saw that far down on the left, close to the area that became swamp, the bank dipped and was noticeably lower than where I perched. Unfortunately, the base of it was submerged, the moonlit creek lapping against it.

I climbed down and carried the ladder into a foot of water, gritting my teeth all the way. After stabilizing the ladder on the rough bottom and climbing to the top, I found I had gained only six inches on the bank. I pulled hard with my arms, my legs and elbows grinding into the sandy bank, and finally heaved myself onto the grass.

Standing up, I brushed off and climbed the hill toward a stand of trees that screened the house from the land below it. On the other side of the trees I was surprised to find a pond, obviously man-made, a perfect oval, a flawless mirror reflecting the three-quarter moon. With an entire creek below, I wondered why the Fairfaxes had bothered to put in an artificial pond.

They must really love their privacy, I thought. Then I remembered a story about wealthy people who stocked their ponds with exotic fish that they and their friends could enjoy catching. That's when it struck me, not like a bolt of lightning out of the blue, more like a fish falling on my foot: the speckled one in the freezer, the one that didn't look like the others Uncle Will had caught, the one that had disappeared recently. I started to laugh. What if Uncle Will had been poaching? What if, winter and summer, when the Fairfax family moved on to their other fabulous homes, he had come here to fish?

And what if someone else had made the connection and removed the evidence that Uncle Will hung out here? I stopped laughing. My eyes moved from the pond to the dark hedge set back from it. I couldn't take my eyes off the hedge, a tall wall of clipped bushes, forty or fifty feet long. Its top, traced in moonlight, was artfully cut to form notches, like those in the battlements of a castle. My eyes dropped down to the base, where a rectangle was cut through the greenery: the doorway I had passed through two times in the last ten days. I glanced back at the pond and shivered. When the owners were gone, this was more than a peaceful spot to fish; it was a perfect place for murder.

Who knew that Uncle Will came here? Aunt Iris, and Audrey, even Elliot Gill could have known. Anyone who happened to be on the water at the right time might have seen Uncle Will arrive in his boat, especially if this was a regular habit of his. The police had found the boat adrift some distance down the creek. It had probably been cut free by his killer, so the police wouldn't guess where my uncle had been fishing. Of course, it was possible that, as longtime neighbors, Will and Iris knew a way onto the estate that I hadn't found; Audrey, too, as a former employee.

I passed through the door in the shrubbery and found myself in an enclosed garden, the hedge and two brick walls making three sides of the square area, the house making the fourth. Lights flicked on, outside lights—there was probably a motion sensor. I stood in the shadow of the hedge for several minutes, studying the house. Every window was dark. If there was a resident caretaker, it was likely that his windows faced the swampy or wooded sides, rather than the scenic view of pond, garden, and creek.

I surveyed the garden, which was divided by crushed stone paths into four sections with a gazebo at the center. "Well, hello," I said softly. To my right was a human-size rabbit, shrubbery sculpted into a tall rabbit with a humanlike stance. Next to him was another tall bush pruned into the figure of a cat, and on the other side of the garden were two more topiary figures, a caterpillar that appeared to be sitting on a mushroom and some kind of rodent—a dormouse, of course! He belonged, along with the Cheshire cat, white rabbit, and caterpillar, to *Alice in Wonderland.*

It was a children's garden and, like a deserted playground, it felt lonely. While summer was in bloom everywhere else in Wisteria, these flower beds had only the headless stalks and papery leaves of dead spring flowers. I walked the garden paths, pausing to study the rabbit and the cat. Rabbit and cat! Amazed at finding the place that had figured in my O.B.E., I had momentarily forgotten about Joanna's words: *The snake slides past a rabbit, glides past a cat.* The images she had "seen" could have been drawn from here. Topiary gardens, requiring years of pruning to create, were maintained for decades and longer. It was possible that this garden had been kept by Mick Sanchez.

Walking the perimeter of the garden with Joanna's images swirling in my mind, I tripped. A hose had been left out, a long rubber snake with a metal head pointing to the gazebo. I turned and strolled toward the wooden structure.

The gazebo had been designed like a child's playhouse. Four of its six sides had windows with shutters, each shutter carved with a heart. The other two sides, one facing the house, and its opposite, facing the entrance through the hedge, had doorways with a carved heart above each of them. I mounted the four steps up to the gazebo and stood inside, pivoting slowly, looking out at the garden. From this focal point, the pattern formed by each quadrant of dried stalks became clear: hearts.

Child-size chairs were pushed over to one side of the

structure. I glanced down, then clicked on my flashlight to survey the floor. A film of dirt and pollen covered the portion facing the house, but the section facing the door in the hedge, and the steps down from it, had been washed clean. I was about to turn off my light when I noticed a deep groove in the wood flooring. I traced it: a square, a door to storage beneath the gazebo. Was this my "rabbit hole," part of my—and Uncle Will's—route to the fire site?

It was easy to imagine a murder scenario: Uncle Will holding his fishing rod, gazing peacefully at the pond, struck on the back of the head by someone he never saw coming; Uncle Will being dragged from the pond, through the hedge, past the topiary rabbit; Uncle Will's body stored beneath the gazebo, the murderer waiting for a way to dispose of it. I figured that the hose had been used to wash down the bloody track left behind.

Although I had followed the path of Uncle Will's murder during my O.B.E., I didn't think I had actually been present at his death. I would have sensed someone else on the paths of this garden, the way I had sensed the crowd on the night of the fire. Somehow, for some reason, Uncle Will chose to lead me along the path he had traveled from his death to the fire. I gazed down at the door to the storage area. There could be evidence here: hair, threads from clothing, a weapon, somthing. I knelt down.

Feeling around the edge of the door, I found an indentation that allowed me to slip my fingers under the boards and lift.

I stared in horror. The beam of my flashlight illuminated the lower end of a leg. The victim's foot was bare, the skin pale and splotchy. My stomach heaved, and I thought I was going to throw up. Then the foot moved.

Twenty-three

"AUNT IRIS. WHAT are you doing in there?"

She slowly shifted position, her face edging out of the shadow created by the gazebo's flooring. "Get in."

"No way," I said.

"You must get in."

She reached up to grasp my arm. I pulled back.

"You must do what I say."

"I won't."

I shone my light into the dark hole, but I couldn't tell how big it was or what it contained. Aunt Iris's eyes shone back at me with a peculiar light. I wasn't sure if I was gazing into the eyes of a psychic or a madwoman. All I knew was that I didn't want to be the next one to die.

"Then you must get in, Anna."

She'd spoken as if she had heard my thoughts, and she had called me Anna. The floodlights, which I had triggered earlier and which had begun to dim, suddenly flashed on again. *Someone else is here,* I thought.

Iris gripped my arms, pulling with all her strength. "If harm comes to you, William will never forgive me. Get in!"

The floodlights went off quickly, not fading, the way they had before. There was no time to reason through the situation. I climbed into the hole with her and lowered the door.

The area beneath the gazebo was about three feet deep and appeared to extend to the edges of the structure.

"Put out your light," Aunt Iris said. "It'll shine through the cracks."

I did so with great reluctance. The moist earth smelled strong, a mix of something cloyingly sweet—mulch, I thought—and something rotten that I couldn't identify.

Aunt Iris heard me sniffing. "What do you smell?"

"I—I don't know. It's cold in here."

"He can't help it."

I did not find it reassuring that she believed Uncle Will was in there with us. After all that had happened, I was no longer certain that only the things I saw existed. I sat hunched, the wetness of the earth seeping through my shorts. When I rested my hands on the dirt beneath me, it felt sticky. Blood-soaked, I thought.

"His blood has dried," Aunt Iris assured me.

"Dried here?"

"Yes. Be quiet. She's coming."

"Who?"

"Quiet!"

My ears strained to hear something. Minutes ticked by. No one came. Still, something was going on with the outside lights.

"Aunt Iris, why are you hiding in here?" I whispered.

"I don't exactly know."

Oh, great, I thought.

"I knew I had to come here, just as you and she had to come here, but I don't know which one of us is drawing the other two."

I repeated her words in my head, trying to tease out their meaning.

"Anna?" The voice came from beyond the gazebo, from the direction of the house. "Anna, where are you? Are you all right?"

Breathing a sigh of relief, I pressed my fingertips against the boards above us to open the door. Aunt Iris's powerful hands grasped mine and pulled them down.

"It's Marcy," I said.

"Of course it is!" she hissed.

"But—" I stopped. My aunt's tone of voice was that of a frustrated teacher speaking to a student who was slow to catch on. I struggled to piece together events.

I had left a note for Zack. Marcy had probably read it. She considered me her responsibility. She probably had keys to the property, knew the gate code, and—no, wait—I hadn't told Zack I was coming here. I hadn't even mentioned borrowing the boat.

"She'll look in here," Iris whispered. "Push back as far as you can from the opening. I'll go out and talk to her."

I heard footsteps on the gravel. Marcy was approaching the gazebo, walking more slowly as she drew closer. Aunt Iris gave me a final shove with her bare foot, raised the trapdoor, and climbed out.

"Well, look who it is." Marcy's voice had a strange flatness to it; I couldn't tell if she was surprised.

"Hello, Marcy. I was expecting you."

"What are you doing here?"

"Same thing as you are," Aunt Iris replied.

"I don't think so."

"Cleaning up," Aunt Iris went on. "You've been sloppy, leaving the hose out, washing only half the gazebo floor. I hope you properly disposed of the weapon."

"I did."

"And his fishing gear?"

"Temporarily, but I will take care of it. Thomas isn't due back from his vacation for another week. No one's minding the place, so there was no need to hurry. Nor was it possible—I've had my hands full, keeping track of Anna."

"I want you to leave her alone, Marcy."

"Do you, now? Don't tell me, you've become fond of her!" There was something creepy about Marcy's voice—an artificial cheerfulness. Then it darkened. "You foolish old woman, don't you realize why Anna has come?"

"Because William died."

"Because William was applying for guardianship of you. We have discussed this a hundred times. Once he had guardianship, he would have legal control over your money—"

"I'm not listening to you," Iris said defiantly.

"Control over where and how you live, control over your health care—"

"I'm not listening!"

"Control over your entire life. And once he did, he and Anna would arrange to have you committed."

"No!"

"He did it before," Marcy reminded her. "Or have you forgotten those days with your special, sniffling, filthy-haired friends?"

"William promised he'd take care of me."

"Of course. Of course he'd take care of you, by shipping you off to an asylum."

"No! He promised he wouldn't do that again. He—he swore it." Aunt Iris's voice, confident when the argument started, had begun to waver.

"It wouldn't require much effort," Marcy continued calmly, "not with his legal power and a bright young niece to support his claims. That's why you killed him, isn't it?"

"I didn't."

"Tell the truth," Marcy challenged.

"I *didn't*!" Aunt Iris insisted, but her denial melted to a rough whisper. "At least, I don't remember doing it."

"You let it happen," Marcy replied. "You knew I would try and you let me. Just like you let me kill Joanna."

I shoved my fist in my mouth to keep any sound from escaping.

"I didn't want you to," Iris argued. "I didn't mean for you to."

"What else could you have intended? You told me Joanna was using her gift, figuring out how Mick died," Marcy said. "It wasn't a matter of what you didn't want to happen but, rather, what you wanted more: whatever was best for your little girl. I'll always be your little girl. You'll always love me best, Mommy Iris." Marcy's childlike lisp turned my skin to gooseflesh. "So, where is Anna?" she asked softly.

"I don't know."

"But you know what has to be done, don't you, Mommy Iris? Perhaps you foresaw it."

"I can't stand any more killing!"

"Anna is piecing together our story, and she is not going to give up on it. There's some family resemblance between her and me. We have the same approach to life's little challenges, and I have found that unexpectedly enjoyable. It's unfortunate that we both can't survive this."

"I can't stand the voices!" Iris cried. "I can't endure any more ghosts!"

"Close your eyes, Mommy Iris, and you won't see them."

"I will always see them," Iris replied. "Only a—a psychotic, heartless person would not."

There was a moment of silence, followed by a sound that made my muscles tighten, a soft, fleshy thump.

"Don't!" Aunt Iris cried. "Don't!"

I pushed open the trapdoor. Aunt Iris lay sprawled on the ground. Marcy, with her hand still raised, turned quickly. "Pop goes the weasel."

"If you've hurt her . . . ," I warned, starting toward Aunt Iris.

"I find it touching the way you two have bonded."

The pale skin of Iris's left cheek was darkening with a bruise, and the corner of her mouth oozed blood. I tried to raise her, but she was dazed, unable to sit up without my arm around her.

If I ran for help, I'd have to leave her behind.

"There was no need to come to her rescue," Marcy told me, resentment seeping into her voice. "I wouldn't kill my own mother."

"You killed your father," I replied. "The image in my mother's reading referred to you. You were the seed of Mick that produced a snake rather than a flower."

"He hated me."

"You killed him in the car accident. The snake was masked. I don't know how you pulled it off, but his death only appeared to be a heart attack."

Marcy laughed her bright, tinkly laugh. "Oh, it was a genuine coronary. Mick took heart medicine. I changed his pills for something a bit more exciting."

She spoke in the same light and informative way as she did when explaining trends in holiday ornaments. Not a hair of her smoothly styled cut was out of place. Her pressed shirt was tucked neatly into casual pants. Did she have a weapon? The night was too warm, I thought, to be wearing that jacket.

"It was so easy," Marcy went on. "I knew they wouldn't do an autopsy, not in this backwoods place, not on a man with a serious heart condition whom everyone seemed to like too much to kill. The lack of bleeding after the accident confirmed their belief that he had died of a heart attack just prior to it."

While talking, she moved herself between the garden exit and Aunt Iris and me, trapping us. I looked back at the house. Marcy must have entered the garden through the large double doors; it appeared that one was open, but it was dark inside. I thought about the way the outside lights were instantly extinguished: Had she cut the electric power? Did she know how to turn off the security alarm? If I ran through the house, would the front gates open?

"Mick was an interfering old fool," Marcy continued, "spying on me and telling my parents every little thing I did. They came to hate me, thanks to him."

I needed to keep her talking while I sorted out my options. And I needed to separate myself from Aunt Iris. She could sit up on her own now.

"I don't see how one employee could make parents hate their child."

"True enough. My adoptive parents were inclined that way from the beginning—or rather, from the time my brother was born. Once they held in their arms the spitting image of a blond Fairfax, they wanted me out of their lives. They stuck me in a corner with Audrey. And they spoiled my brother—they gave him things that I should have had."

"Like what?" I asked, but she didn't need encouragement.

"Whenever I got the opportunity, I took back. I took my

share. Then Mick would go running to them, tattling on me."

"Maybe he was trying to help," I said, defending him, baiting her. "You were his child, and he wanted you to grow up right. I think it was Mick's way of loving."

"He feared me! I could see it in his eyes. He hated and feared me, and he persuaded everyone else to, with one exception: Audrey." I heard the scorn in her voice. "Mick hadn't a clue how to handle Audrey."

"But you did," I replied. "You're good at manipulating people."

"Thank you."

I hadn't meant it as a compliment. "It's you, not Aunt Iris, who needs to be committed. You're crazy."

She laughed. "Well, I'm certainly not *psychic*. And you know the choice that we O'Neill women have."

Psychic or psychotic. Uncle Will had known that too. The child whom he and Aunt Iris had argued about was Marcy, not me. What he feared had come true: Living close to her child had caused Iris great pain.

"When Uncle Will found my mother's client book, he realized that you had killed Mick. He poached here, and he recognized the images in my mother's psychic reading."

"William always hated me. Last month, when he figured it out, he rather stupidly told Mommy Iris, told her what she already knew. It didn't take much for me to discover why she was suddenly so upset. Have you decided what it is going to be for you?"

I looked at Marcy, puzzled.

"Psychic or psychotic?" she asked, her voice pleasant, as if she were inquiring about a preference for regular or decaf.

Aunt Iris, I said silently, *if you can hear me, I need you to distract Marcy.* Aloud I said, "I don't think a person chooses to be either."

"Perhaps not chooses," Marcy responded, "but allows it, nurtures it."

Aunt Iris, please help me. I need a running start.

"Who's there?" Aunt Iris murmured, turning her head slowly toward the gazebo. Marcy and I followed her gaze. "Is it you, William?" she asked.

It's me, Anna.

"William," Aunt Iris murmured.

No. Anna!

"William, let it rest," she moaned. She moved her head from side to side, grimacing, but kept her eyes fixed on the space above the trapdoor. With the bright moonlight reflecting off the gazebo's roof, its interior looked dark and murky.

"William," she groaned.

Her eyes shimmered in the silver light, then began to rise under the wrinkled tent of her eyelids.

"Stop it!" Marcy said.

"William . . . William . . . William!" Aunt Iris cried, her voice climbing higher each time she spoke. She rocked back and forth.

"William . . . William . . . William!"

The sockets of her eyes shone white, like those of a marble statue.

"Stop it, Mommy Iris!"

Her mouth twitched, stretched, had a life of its own. Then her eyes rolled forward again, and another face, a stranger's face, looked out of my aunt's.

"Stop it now!" Marcy demanded.

Run, Anna.

I blinked. *What?*

The stranger's face retracted, grew back into Aunt Iris's. Her body shuddered, as if she were going to vomit whatever had possessed her.

Run, Anna.

I stared at her in amazement. *This is for me?*

Her mouth stretched again. She looked like a snake about to swallow something larger than itself.

Marcy crouched with fear. "Stop it, Mommy! Stop it!"

Run, Anna, run.

I took off.

Twenty-four

I RACED TOWARD the house and found the door open. Behind me I heard Iris wailing and Marcy shouting at her. How long could Iris keep Marcy distracted? Long enough for me to get to the front door and up the driveway, that's what I needed.

The moment I stepped into the dark house, I remembered that my flashlight was under the gazebo. There was no time to wait for my eyes to adjust to the darkness. I plunged ahead. I didn't know the floor plan, didn't know even the basic shape of the house, having seen only the section of it that backed up to the walled garden. But big houses often had center halls. If the pond and the children's garden were centered, it was likely that I had entered the hall that ran straight to the front door.

I ran straight into a wall. For a moment I was stunned, then I felt the surface in front of me—wood—a door. I groped for a handle. When my fingers touched the metal knob, I wanted to yank open the door, but I forced myself to turn the knob slowly, quietly, then I tiptoed through and closed the door again, just as slowly and quietly, not wanting to call attention to myself.

There wasn't a pencil line of light visible. I moved forward steadily, trying to walk straight, my hands out in front of me. I felt as if I had stumbled into a room the size of a gymnasium. In a house like this, the rooms could be large, I thought, and so could the halls.

I heard footsteps. Marcy had entered the house. I heard her walking in the room behind the door. I fought the urge to race through the house: I was a mouse in a pitch-black maze being pursued by a cat who knew the maze by heart. The moment I made a noise, I had better be close to an exit. I moved steadily forward, listening for Marcy, wondering why she didn't burst through the door between us.

Because she knew other doors, other ways to get to me, I thought. She wasn't going to give herself away, not until she had me where she could strike quickly and easily—from behind, her favorite method.

I kept walking. My legs felt strange and rubbery. With each step, my sense of direction became less certain. My hand touched something that felt like wood and was shaped like a thick rod. I felt to the right and left of it—the spindles of a staircase. The banister they supported was wide, like that of the main stairway of a large house. But the stairs weren't straight ahead. They didn't point to what I had hoped was the front door, or maybe they did and I had veered off course. I was confused.

Having nothing else to follow, I followed the stairway wall, losing track of the steps as they rose. I came to another wall with a door in it. Finding the knob, I turned it quietly, pushed against the door, and stepped through. I lurched forward, hanging on to the door handle and swinging wildly. Another set of steps. The door had saved me from tumbling headlong down them.

Regaining my balance, I took one step down and groped in vain for a railing. The walls on either side of me were close, like those of a stairway down to a basement, but the air didn't smell like a cellar's. I took two more steps, then jammed my foot against a level floor.

I was just four steps down, in a wing of the house, I thought. Wings were often smaller, at least in the historic houses I had seen; I reasoned that it would be easier to find an exit. I'd do it methodically, feeling my way around a room till I found a window. I quietly shut the door to my wing and moved along the hallway.

I felt a door frame and turned right, assuming that I was in the first room of the wing. I kept thinking I'd see a crack of moonlight somewhere, but it was so dark, I couldn't see the hand in front of my face.

Starting with the wall immediately to my right, I felt a smooth wood surface and a vertical groove, then another smooth surface and another groove: paneling. I worked my way around a chair, then past a corner, continuing till my hand touched a wood ridge. My fingers followed the ridge up to a shelf about chin high and surprisingly long. I tripped on a rough surface: a fireplace. *An outside wall!* I thought triumphantly, then remembered that some houses had chimneys inside. I bumped into a table placed next to the fireplace and, taking a half step back from it, moved sideways till I reached a second corner in the room.

I turned the corner and prayed for a window. At last my hands grasped loose fabric. I felt behind it, shoving back what seemed like yards of material. The walls of the house were thick, the windowsill deep. My fingers searched for cool panes of glass but touched wood—a set of inside shutters. I felt for the center, tried unsuccessfully to pry the pair open, then ran my hands up and down the crack, hunting for a fastener. My fingers grasped a knob, and I pulled on it. It wouldn't budge. I felt around the knob and discovered a metal circle with a jagged edge inside. *Terrific!*—they had locks on their shutters, locks that required keys. This place was secure, even with the electricity off.

I sagged against the deep windowsill for a moment, then straightened up and listened, my attention caught by a sound that seemed to come from behind the fireplace. A heavy object was being dragged across the floor in the room behind the one I was in.

I should have realized then that if Marcy was ignoring me, it was because she had something more important to do at the moment. I should have stopped to think things through. But when someone has made it clear she wants to kill you, the instinct to flee pushes out all other thoughts, and you keep moving.

After the window, I reached the corner quickly, which indicated I was in a small room. Turning the corner, I felt a built-in bookcase, shelves with binders and folders. Expecting nothing but office materials, I got careless. My hand suddenly struck something tall and smooth to the touch. It crashed into the furniture behind me and shattered. Through the fireplace wall, I heard a loud, raucous laugh. Marcy knew where I was now. I backed into a chair and desk, turned myself around, and headed toward what I thought was the room's exit.

I was back in the hall. I knew because when I took an extra step to the left or right, I could touch the walls. I felt the frame of a doorway and entered the next room, walking straight ahead this time, hoping for windows. I banged my shin on a low table. It was all I could do not to kick it aside. I had passed the point of daunting fear and was getting reckless and desperate. Then

I heard the sound of a door opening, the door into the wing. Marcy was coming for me. I moved quickly around the room, hoping for a window with unlocked shutters. I prayed to God and to Uncle Will. I groped and found the mantel of another fireplace.

"Where are you, baby?"

Baby?

I felt for the tools usually kept by a hearth. There were none.

"Are we playing hide-and-seek, baby?" Marcy's voice sounded high-pitched, peculiar.

I kept searching for something to defend myself with. Next to the fireplace my hand grasped a knob. I pulled on it— *Yes! Stairs!* Maybe the second-floor windows weren't locked. I tiptoed up two steps and reached back to close the door behind me.

"All right, I will count, and you hide." Her voice chilled me to the bone. "O-one, two-oo, three . . ."

I scurried up the turning steps, hoping the door hiding the stairway and her loud counting would muffle the noise I made. At the top of the steps I stopped to remove my shoes so she wouldn't hear me walking above her head.

I stood still for a moment, trying to orient myself, which was impossible since it was as dark upstairs as down. I didn't understand the lower floor plan, so I couldn't imagine a duplicate much less a variation of it for the second floor. But I did know I was in a wing, and if I found a short stairway, it would indicate that I was moving back toward the center of the house. If Marcy came up the turning stair and I could find the main stair, I'd be able to race down it and, with a little luck, find the front door or the exit to the garden.

I started toward what I thought would be the center portion of the house. Marcy had stopped counting. I heard a noise, footsteps in a different place than I had expected hers to be.

"Anna?"

Zack! It was Zack's voice, calling from below.

"Anna? Anna!" he cried.

I had to bite my tongue to keep from shouting back. Marcy was silent, listening. If I answered Zack, she'd know where I was. But if I didn't warn him, she might lie in wait for him. Two against one, we had a chance; somehow, Zack and I had to find each other.

I prayed. *Help. Help me know where he is.*

Zack had become quiet, as if he had figured out the nature of the game being played. The silence of the house was like a roaring in my ears.

Maybe I could send my mind out, I thought, send it on a journey like I did during an O.B.E. Guessing that Zack had entered the house the same way as I had, I imagined the room off the garden, picturing in my head how I would move along its walls, searching it with mental hands.

There was a door—not the door I had gone through, a door to the left. *Are you there, Zack? Yes!* I knew it in the place I call my "heart." And then he wasn't. I had lost him.

He's moving, I thought. *I have to keep up with him.* But at that moment I heard a sound close to where I was standing, the turn of a knob. Marcy was opening the door to the steps I had just climbed.

I rushed ahead, then smashed my toes into a step and sprawled forward, catching another step with spread palms—the top step, I realized—a short stairway into the main portion of the house. Scrambling up it, I heard Marcy climbing the turning stairs.

"Where are you now, baby?" Marcy called. "Are you hidden? Hide-and-seek."

I shivered at the childish pitch of her voice and tiptoed forward.

"Have you found a good spot, baby? Here I come, ready or not."

Why was she calling me "baby"? Did she think I was her brother? Was this a game she had played with her hated younger sibling? She was crazy.

I waved my arms around, hoping to touch a surface. I felt as if tricks were being played on me, as if the walls had the power to recede from me when I reached out. *Get a grip, Anna.* Maybe I was in a large, square hall. *Then I must be near the steps,* I thought.

Stop, let your mind search, I told myself, but I couldn't. I didn't trust myself enough to stand still and let my mind do the work.

"I'm coming, baby. I'm going to find you."

My left hand finally touched a wall, and I raced ahead, letting my fingers drag lightly along to keep me going straight. A doorway—I hesitated. There was no light inside the room: The shutters were closed on this floor as well. I kept going. Another doorway, another pitch-black room. I slipped inside and flattened my back against the wall by the door. *Stop, think,* I told myself; *you're going to get yourself cornered.*

I took deep breaths, trying to slow my racing thoughts. My mind went out into the hall again—I sent it there. I searched for Zack: He was coming upstairs. *Zack. Zack, I'm here.*

I heard Marcy opening and closing doors in the wing I had come from. "Olly olly in free," she sang out, as if calling in the players of her game. I wondered if she knew, as I did, that Zack was climbing toward the upstairs hall.

He's at the top of the main stairway, I thought. The stairs ran sideways, not back to front, as I had assumed. I must have rushed past its landing without realizing it.

He was in the hall now, coming toward me. I started out of the room, moving as fast as I could while trying to be quiet, wanting to reach Zack quickly and get us both back to the steps he had just climbed. His light was off, but I knew where he was. I extended my arm and touched him. He jumped.

Something clattered to the floor—his flashlight. In response, a wild laugh erupted from Marcy.

"It's Anna," I whispered.

Zack gripped my hand. "We've got to get out of here."

But Marcy had come racing from the wing and positioned herself at the top of the main stairs, blocking our escape route. I saw it as she shone her flashlight on us. Zack used the brightness of her light to find the one he had dropped. He clicked the button, and for a moment they focused their beams on each other.

"I see you," she said, her eyes sparkling in the light. She shook her head, her perfectly cut hair swinging a bit. She was like a child who had discovered the feel of her hair moving and enjoyed making it do that. "You are supposed to hide! Hide, hide now. I'll count again."

"She's off the deep end," I said to Zack.

"No kidding."

Marcy played at hiding her eyes. "O-one, two-oo, three . . ."

"Does she own a gun?" I asked.

"She wouldn't have told me if she does."

"We'll never get past her. We need to find another stairway."

"Or try a window. What's in here?" He shone his flashlight around the room from which I had just emerged.

"The shutters are locked. At least, they are downstairs," I told him.

"I'll break them open."

"There's probably another set of back stairs. They're usually next to a fireplace," I said, placing my hand over his to guide the beam of light, scanning the walls on either side of the hearth. "I'm going next door."

"Better stay together," he said. "If this battery gives out—"

"I can find you."

He started banging at the shutters' lock, using his metal flashlight like a hammer. Out in the hall Marcy was reciting her numbers in a singsong voice that set my teeth on edge. I stepped into the hall, then froze.

Marcy had set her flashlight on its side, and it illuminated her, throwing tall shadows against the walls. While counting cheerfully, she poured a liquid across the landing of the main stairs, then moved swiftly to the entrance to the wing, still pouring.

"Do you smell that?" Zack asked from inside the room.

"I see it. She's going to burn this place down."

Zack hurried to the door and watched her a moment. "Crazy, but not stupid—one more arson. You've got to help me break through this shutter. There must be back stairs, but if we don't find them—"

He picked up a wood chair with a long back and four thick legs. We lined up, making the chair a battering ram, and ran at the window, jamming the chair legs into the shutter. Pieces of wood splintered and broke off. We ran at it again.

"She's lit something," he said, and rushed to the door to close it.

It was eerie, smelling the fire again, smelling it as I had the night I was with my uncle. I began to yank on the heavy curtains, and Zack, realizing why, joined me, using his weight to bring down the drapes.

He handed them to me, and I rushed them to the door to stuff under the crack, hoping to keep out deadly smoke. "Want this rod?"

"Yes. No. The andiron!" he said. He picked up one of the heavy brass pieces intended to hold logs. Looking like a shot-putter, he spun to gain momentum, then slammed the andiron against the shutters. The lock snapped. I ran to the window, and both of us clawed at the wooden panels, opening them. We struggled with the window locks, then shoved up the sash.

I heard a whoosh. Drapes or not, the house was too old to

be airtight, and we had created a draft. Marcy screamed, then let out an excited laugh. "Here I come, ready or not."

"I hope you're not afraid of heights," Zack said.

"I'm more afraid of fire." But when I looked down from the window, I saw that the large proportions of the house had put us farther off the ground than I expected.

"It's okay," Zack said, as if sensing my fear. "Get in the window. It's wide enough for both of us." He climbed through first, then gripped my arm as I climbed into a sitting position. I sat on the sill, clinging to the bottom of the raised window.

Zack shone his flashlight on the shrubs below. The blue of the LED, like the moonlight, reflected off the surface of bushes. They were mounded deep against the house.

"Want me to go first?" he asked. When I didn't reply, he said, "Okay, we'll jump at the same time."

I pressed my lips together and forced myself to nod.

He studied my face. "This is like the water-at-night thing," he said, remembering our conversation at the party. "You don't like it because you can't see what's beneath the surface. Want me to go first?" When I still didn't answer, he said, "I'll go first, but you've got to jump right after. Promise?"

"Promise."

He leaped.

I watched him roll far below me, lie still for a moment,

then stagger to his feet. He rushed forward, shook the bushes in a rough kind of search, then called up. "No thorns, no stakes, no skunks. And you don't have to worry about the lawn sprinkler—it's sticking out of my back. Just kidding. Jump, Anna!"

I nodded and turned myself around until I lay with my belly on the windowsill.

"Anna, what are you doing?" Zack cried.

"Getting five feet closer to the ground." I planned to hang by my hands, then close my eyes and drop. But at that moment the door of the room burst open.

Marcy came through, and I saw in one terrifying flash the hallway burning behind her. She started toward me. I quickly lowered myself till I dangled by my hands. I couldn't see her, but I could hear her gasping, coughing uncontrollably from the poisonous smoke.

"Marcy," I called, "crawl, crawl to the window!" I beat my feet against the house, trying to get traction, trying to hoist myself back up.

"Anna, drop!" Zack shouted.

"Marcy, come on. *Come here!*" I pulled myself up high enough for my chin to be supported by the sill. I saw that the fire was burning fast, coming into the room.

"Marcy, crawl to me!"

She sat on the floor wheezing. I didn't have the strength in my arms to pull myself all the way up.

"Marcy, can you hear me? Crawl to me! Crawl to the window! *Please!*"

"Anna!" Zack shouted.

"Marcy!" I screamed, desperate to get through to her. The fire was a quarter of the way into the room, close to the edge of the rug.

She looked up suddenly, her light eyes meeting mine. The hungry flames were within two feet of her. She laughed in a manner too bright and tinkly for an adult. "Better fire here than fire hereafter," Marcy said, and leaned back.

"Let go, Anna," Zack begged from below.

Let go, Anna, Uncle Will called.

Let go, Anna. The third voice was soft, familiar, sounding closer than if the words had been spoken in my ear.

"Mother Joanna?"

Let go now, she said.

And I did.

Twenty-five

SHOCK—THE NUMBNESS of it, the disconnect it creates with actual events—is useful. It keeps you from running through a burning house, screaming to the person left behind, when it is much too late.

Zack and I crawled together out of the bushes, then ran fifty feet or more before turning back to look at the house. Aunt Iris emerged from the main entrance. She must have taken the route I had been looking for so desperately. The fire roaring above her and its choking smell did not seem to faze her. *Shock,* I thought, and called to her. She came quietly.

Aunt Iris, Zack, and I sat together on the wet grass and watched the upper story burn, listening to the approaching sirens, thinking about Marcy.

I remember the next two hours as a jumble of images: the pulsating lights of the trucks; the smoke that kept pouring out when there were no more flames; the look on Dave's face; the way Zack held his father in his arms and cried with him. We waited for the firefighters to remove Marcy's remains, but with the effort now designated as recovery rather than rescue, and her body considered part of a crime scene, the police told us it would be hours before that happened.

I put my arms around Aunt Iris. She had borne the burden of Marcy for years, and in some ways, her burden had finally been lifted. Now Zack's father was bearing the brunt of the pain. My eyes met Zack's. I ached for him and Dave.

We left Aunt Iris's car where she had parked it earlier, in the employee lot on the estate. She told the sheriff she had "sensed" the gate's entry code, but I thought it just as likely that Marcy had divulged it at some point. McManus's deputy drove us home, then stayed and drank some stale instant coffee. Later I found out he had been told not to question us. I was grateful to the sheriff; while I could have insisted on having a lawyer present, there was no controlling what Aunt Iris might say with or without legal advice. She wandered from room to room, and I held my breath, hoping she would not talk to the grandfather clock or smash a mirror. She didn't, and the young deputy never ventured out of our kitchen.

At three a.m., Sheriff McManus arrived, accompanied by a fire investigator and Zack. Earlier Zack had called his uncle, who had made the drive from Philadelphia and was now with Dave.

In a quiet discussion on the porch, I told them that Marcy had admitted to killing Mick, my mother, and Uncle Will, and that the police should look for forensic evidence of the third murder beneath the gazebo. I assumed she had killed Uncle Will while he was fishing on the estate and that Uncle Will's equipment might be found nearby. I then asked what I needed to know most: If it "happened" that Aunt Iris had "suspicions" about Marcy's crimes, would she face charges? The sheriff said his unprofessional opinion was that mental incompetency would get her off the hook but that I needed to phone her attorney and have her present when he questioned her. He also advised me of my rights.

Returning to the kitchen, I suggested to Aunt Iris that she go up to her room and rest. She was exhausted and didn't fight me on it. Then the four of us sat down to piece together the story of that evening.

At 7:15, Zack had driven Erika to an appointment with McManus and the fire investigator, having convinced her that if she didn't come clean, he would go to the authorities himself. When Zack had stood guard outside the house Friday and discovered the obsessive Elliot Gill watching the upstairs windows, he didn't know what to think, except that the facts of the arson game had to be revealed immediately so that the police could figure things out before another tragedy occurred.

Returning home from his and Erika's meeting with authorities, Zack found that his father was still at a business dinner, but, unknown to Zack, Marcy had come home and read my note. Audrey, ever watchful for evil acts, had observed and happily reported to Marcy that I had stolen Zack's boat and headed up-creek. Marcy must have guessed where I was going and realized I was giving her a golden opportunity to get rid of me.

She instructed Audrey not to tell Zack that I had come for him. Later the note I had written was found in Marcy's purse. It was Zack's theory that Marcy had planned to give the note to the police and tell them about my previous assault. Erika's three friends had unwittingly provided Marcy with cover for another murder. It wasn't clear when Marcy's final plan for me came together. As the fire investigator pointed out, quantities of accelerants are readily available in country houses, and Marcy was familiar with her childhood home.

Audrey did not tell Zack about the note, but, fortunately for me, she couldn't resist telling him about the stolen boat. Setting out in his father's cruiser, Zack had spotted the anchored rowboat, then the ladder that I'd left against the bank. Following my route, he had found Iris semiconscious in the garden. At that point he called 911 on his cell.

When Zack entered the house, he still didn't understand what was happening. While aware that his stepmother visited Iris occasionally, he had not known the nature of their relationship and had no idea why Marcy would hurt Iris or Will. But when he heard her counting in her strange game of hide-and-seek, he knew Marcy was dangerous. He feared it was his own text messages that had been accessed, that it was Marcy who had used Erika's game as a convenient cover for Uncle Will's murder.

That was as much as we could get through that night—or that morning, I should say. The sheriff told us all to get some sleep. He planned to get his own shut-eye in his car, which he had parked across the top of Aunt Iris's driveway, protecting us from curious intruders. Zack needed to get home to Dave. On his way out, he stopped for just a moment, his fingers brushing the tips of mine.

I went to check on Aunt Iris. Her room was dark, but she was up, sitting on the edge of her bed. "I can't sleep."

I turned on a soft lamp and sat on a chair close to her bed.

"They made me promise I wouldn't tell her," Aunt Iris said. Her eyes were wide open, but when I looked in them, I didn't think she was seeing the present.

"You mean the Fairfaxes."

"They broke their promise, the one they made to me when

I gave them Marcy. So I broke mine. After they had the boy—after they decided Marcy didn't matter anymore—I told her she was mine."

I could imagine how it had happened. Whether Marcy was emotionally abandoned by her parents or whether she was simply a spoiled child with a bad case of sibling jealousy, all Iris could see was her own child suffering.

And what had Uncle Will seen? The outcome that he had feared all along, knowing Iris's unstable mind and a mother's strong feelings for her child.

"William argued with me when I was pregnant, said the Fairfaxes lived too close."

I wondered silently why the Fairfaxes weren't wary of the O'Neill reputation; perhaps the gossip was a more recent phenomenon, or perhaps the Fairfaxes didn't mix enough with the locals to hear it.

"I thought he meant it would be too painful for me. I didn't know it would hurt other people."

I said nothing, unable to respond in a way that would comfort her. I didn't remember Joanna or the pain her death had caused me as a toddler. The only mother that I remembered loved me still, and I loved her. But Uncle Will's death cut deep.

"I didn't tell Marcy who her father was, not while he was alive."

"Did Audrey know?"

She shook her head no. "Marcy was born here at the house. Since Mick wouldn't admit she was his child, he couldn't tell me what to do with her, couldn't tell the Fairfaxes not to take her. Marcy and Mick never got along. He was hard on her."

"Maybe he was afraid for her."

"*Of* her," Aunt Iris corrected. "He was afraid of her the way he was afraid of me."

More afraid, I thought, seeing a selfishness and greed in Marcy that wasn't in Aunt Iris. I wondered at what point Uncle Will had bought the book *Psychosis and the Criminal Mind*. I suspected that it was to understand Marcy rather than Iris.

"When Mick died, a part of me knew that Marcy had done it. Joanna didn't suspect at first—didn't know my relationship to Marcy or Mick—she simply wanted to help Audrey. I tried to stop her, but she wouldn't listen to me. So I told Marcy that Joanna was reading Mick's psychic signs and she should get out of Wisteria for a while. I never expected she'd kill Joanna. I couldn't allow myself to think that Marcy would kill someone as sweet and loving as Joanna."

I swallowed hard.

Iris sat on the edge of her bed, rocking back and forth, hands clasped tightly in her lap. "What could I do? What could I do? I couldn't bear to lose my daughter, too. And reporting Marcy wasn't going to bring back Joanna. 'She won't do it again,' I thought. 'There's no reason for her to.'"

"But there was," I interjected. "She'd kill as long as she needed to, to save her own skin."

"I'm sorry. I'm sorry," Aunt Iris said.

I couldn't say, *That's okay. I forgive you.* I couldn't say that yet.

"I'm sorry," she repeated plaintively.

"I know you are. Try to get some rest."

Twenty-six

IN THE DAYS that followed, Zack and I had our hands full. His father had lost more than his wife and their future together: With the information that surfaced about Marcy, Dave's memories of the person he had loved were destroyed. My aunt lost the daughter she had spent thirty-seven years protecting. As for Audrey, as much as I disliked her self-righteousness, I felt sorry for her. She lost her "project" in life, the little girl she had helped to raise and the woman she cared for in later years. She also lost her belief that she had known everything about her husband. Zack and I spent every waking moment trying to support the people who had lost so much as well as working with authorities.

The sheriff also had his hands full. With additional police support, traces of Uncle Will's blood were found in the gazebo. They fingerprinted the smooth, painted rocks that had been placed on my bed in imitation of Audrey's work and found Marcy's prints. I would never know whether Marcy was trying to scare me away or had started on a plan to murder me.

Erika was charged with second-degree arson and malicious destruction of property, and Carl and his two friends—the guys who had attacked me—with assault. Although I didn't like Erika, it was the three guys I found scary. Their excuse for inflicting pain and threatening serious harm was simply that they were "looking out for their own." Carl's two companions were in the process of copping deals, offering information that proved Carl responsible for the earlier harassment of Uncle Will. I guess in their and Marcy's world, it was every man for himself.

By law, the kids who attended the fire and made no effort to stop Erika were also accountable. The sheriff thought they'd end up with probation—a close monitoring of their school and home life—as well as community service. Mom kept reminding me that it was for the best; they needed their parents to pay more attention to what they were into.

Yes, Mom came. And here's the really weird thing: She arrived in Wisteria the day after the fire. The night of the fire she awoke with a bad feeling, and for a reason she couldn't really explain, she started packing suitcases. At seven a.m. she tried to call me, but I had turned off my cell. She tried Aunt Iris's landline next, but by the time I awoke to answer it, she had given up. Not waiting any longer, Mom put the kids and the dog in the car and started for Maryland. Maybe psychic stuff can bypass genetics; maybe it can work heart to heart.

With the arrival of my Baltimore family, Aunt Iris's silent house sprang to life. The girls and I took the room that had been Joanna's and mine, the one with the blue-flowered wallpaper. Jack begged for my corner of the attic. Mom took Uncle Will's room. Rosy slept in the upstairs hall at night, and when she needed some peace, hung out in Uncle Will's den—she liked the brick floor.

To Grace, Claire, and Jack, it seemed as if we had just won the lottery. Suddenly, they had a large house to run through; a backyard as big as a park, which had its own "lake," as they called the creek; and "a castle" next door, the Flemings' home.

Aunt Iris informed me that Uncle Will had departed shortly after she and I had talked in her bedroom, which was just as well, for with my family, there would be no resting in peace in his own home. Surprisingly, Aunt Iris seemed to like the noise; maybe it drowned out some of the noise that was inside her head. Or maybe, with Marcy gone, she was truly more at peace. Rosy liked the new doggy friend she found in Clyde, and Clyde introduced her to the joy of ducks. Aunt Iris's cats could handle both dogs, but they were wary of the kids at first, spending a lot of time on the hood of Uncle Will's pickup.

Dave and Zack often followed Clyde through the gate in the hedge. Dave was selling the house—its memories were too painful—but he seemed to be able to bear up better when he was around us.

As for Zack, he found out what it was like to be adored by little kids. I envied the freedom Claire and Grace felt with him—tackling him in the grass, climbing on his shoulders in the creek, getting him to draw pictures that they could color in. I would have liked to feel his big hand wrap around mine the way it wrapped around theirs. When he was gentle with them, I felt a strange ache inside me.

I even felt a little left out. In Baltimore I had been Jack's pitcher when he batted, his quarterback when he received, and his receiver when he quarterbacked. Now it was always Zack and Jack, and when Jack couldn't pull Zack away from the twins, he trailed behind Dave.

But that wasn't the real problem. With all the people that Zack and I were paying attention to, there didn't seem to be the time or space alone to figure out our own connection. There was a bridge between us, formed by the people we loved, but I didn't know how to cross it. Maybe I didn't have the nerve to.

About two weeks after Marcy's death, when a semblance of normal life had returned, thanks to Mom, I was in the kitchen, sipping a glass of Dr Pepper, taking a break from the book I had been reading on psychic phenomena. I thought I had the gift, and I had been raised to believe we are supposed to use God's gifts, but I wasn't yet confident enough to let go and see what I was capable of. *In time,* as Aunt Iris said.

Mom was putting the kids to bed. I could hear their scampering feet above me. Aunt Iris had gone off in her gold sedan to who knows where, and the cats had wandered away into the trees. I walked down to the dock, stepped over the life vests the kids and I had left there, and sat at the end, swinging my feet over the dark water.

I don't know how long I'd been there when Zack called from the other dock, "Can I come over?"

Before I could reply, he dove into the water, breaking the moonlight into silver pieces. I watched him swim the distance and climb the ladder onto our dock. He sat next to me, his arm dripping on me.

"Anna," he said, "we're good friends, right?"

"Right."

"And good friends are honest with each other, right?"

"Right. . . . Well, most of the time," I said.

He glanced sideways at me and laughed. "I need honest advice."

I waited for him to continue. I wondered how I was ever going to get over him.

"I've got girlfriend problems."

Oh, great, just what I wanted to advise him on. "You

know, Zack, I'm not really good at that kind of stuff."

"But I know you understand, because we talked about it before. You know how some girls are attracted to artist types, while other girls think that's the last thing they need and are interested in jocks?"

I swung my legs. "Yeah."

"I have two girls really interested in me."

I felt like saying, *Just two?*

"I mean *really* interested," he went on. "One of them wants to marry me."

"What?!"

"How do I tell them I'm in love with their sister?"

I turned to him.

"Anna," he said softly, "I am in way over my head with a girl who has chestnut-colored hair. I have been from the beginning. But maybe before I tell the others, I should find out if their sister would give me half a chance. What do you think?"

"I think the others are too young for you," I said. "But the girl with the red hair, she might be just right."

"I know she is."

Our first kiss was shy. The second was longer and sweeter. The third—well, to be honest, on the third kiss I fell off the dock and took him with me. And the dark water wasn't scary at all.

About the Author

A former high school and college teacher with a Ph.D. in English Literature from the University of Rochester, Elizabeth Chandler enjoys visiting schools to talk about the process of creating books. She has written numerous picture books for children under her real name, Mary Claire Helldorfer, as well as romances for teens under her pen name, Elizabeth Chandler. Her romance novels include *Summer in the City*, *Love at First Click*, and the romance-mystery *Kissed by an Angel*, published by Simon Pulse.

When not writing, Mary Claire enjoys biking, gardening, and following the Orioles and Ravens. Mary Claire lives in Baltimore with her husband, Bob, and their cat, Puck.